Praise for *Harold*

"Like *Catcher in the Rye* on mushrooms. Read this damn book. It's a masterpiece. Steven Wright is a genius."

—Bill Burr

"Really funny and touching. *Harold* is beautifully written. Only Steven Wright could write this, and I love it."

—Conan O'Brien

"A strange and wonderful book . . . There are shades of Vonnegut in Wright, and shades of John Irving's Owen Meany in the precocious Harold."

—Michael Ian Black, *The New York Times Book Review*

"If Kurt Vonnegut and *Calvin and Hobbes* creator Bill Watterson wrote a literary version of *Harold and the Purple Crayon*, they might have concocted an absurdist novel like *Harold*. Or maybe, *Harold* could only have come from the off-kilter but fertile musings of stand-up legend Steven Wright . . . His deadpan delivery elevated him to the top of the stand-up world in the 1980s. That same originality and dry humor ricochets throughout his novel."

—Stuart Miller, *The Los Angeles Times*

"*Harold* is often funny . . . as if Donald Barthelme had been assigned to rewrite *The Little Prince*. Wright has invented something here: A story about a child that refuses to be childlike, authored by an author who refuses to pretend that there's order to the disorganized mind of a too-smart kid who can't keep on task."

—Mark Athitakis, *The Washington Post*

"Readers enthralled by stand-up comedian Wright's uniquely brainy, topsy-turvy, metaphysical, and epigrammatic humor will revel in Harold's uncanny, sharply funny, and profound ponderings in this sardonic yet tender tale of life's mysteries and the mind's marvels."

—Donna Seaman, *Booklist*

Harold

A NOVEL

Steven Wright

Simon & Schuster Paperbacks

NEW YORK · LONDON · TORONTO
SYDNEY · NEW DELHI

100 YEARS

**SIMON &
SCHUSTER
PAPERBACKS**

Simon & Schuster
1230 Avenue of the Americas
New York, NY 10020

First Simon & Schuster paperback edition May 2024

SIMON & SCHUSTER and colophon are registered trademarks of Simon & Schuster, LLC

Simon & Schuster: Celebrating 100 Years of Publishing in 2024

For information about special discounts for bulk purchases, please contact Simon & Schuster Special Sales at 1-866-506-1949 or business@simonandschuster.com.

The Simon & Schuster Speakers Bureau can bring authors to your live event. For more information or to book an event, contact the Simon & Schuster Speakers Bureau at 1-866-248-3049 or visit our website at www.simonspeakers.com.

Interior design by Paul Dippolito

Manufactured in the United States of America

1   3   5   7   9   10   8   6   4   2

Library of Congress Cataloging-in-Publication Data has been applied for.

ISBN 978-1-6680-2269-6
ISBN 978-1-6680-2270-2 (pbk)
ISBN 978-1-6680-2271-9 (ebook)

For Barry Crimmins and Peter Lassally

Harold

Chapter 1

Ms. Yuka was standing in front of her desk when she began to brush a small piece of lint off her skirt just above her right knee and Harold wondered if there was more lint in China than in the United States and wondered if it mattered and if so how?

Harold wondered if the Chinese had their own FBI and if it was called the CFBI.

Could the CFBI and the FBI tell the difference between Chinese fingerprints and American fingerprints and he didn't mean a specific person he meant was there an in general difference?

Then he thought there should be a fistfight between the guy who said no two fingerprints were alike and the guy who said no two snowflakes were alike. A fight to the death.

After Ms. Yuka finished with her US/Chinese lint she said to the class:

"Remember to keep working on your book report and your oral presentation which are both due after Christmas vacation which starts Friday."

Harold's book report was about a book he read about Alfred Nobel who was the guy who invented dynamite.

He worked in a factory as a chemist focussing on explosives. His brother worked there too and was accidentally killed in an explosion.

So Alfred decided to turn this horrible tragedy into something positive.

With the huge fortune he made from dynamite he developed the Nobel Prize which led to the Nobel Peace Prize.

Harold thought if this was true what kind of prizes could the guy who invented the atom bomb come up with?

Maybe the "Universe Peace Prize."

Just to torture Ms. Yuka Harold thought of asking her if the book report should be about the subject of the book or a report about how the book was written.

But he didn't because he was tired and just wasn't in the mood.

Harold was 7 in 3rd grade at Wildwood Elementary School.

He did more thinking than someone his age. Or any age.

He thought wouldn't it be great to be able to sleep standing up with your eyes open.

Imagine asking Elizabeth if she would like to meet him some night in the middle of the woods so they could sleep standing up with their eyes open facing each other, and he wondered what kinds of dreams they would have then?

And wouldn't it be weird if they both had dreams but neither one of them was in the other's dreams.

Elizabeth was a girl in the class.

Harold thought that Alfred Nobel should have a fistfight with the guy who invented gunpowder whose name nobody knew because it was invented by the Chinese in the 9th century. A fight to the death.

He wondered if Ms. Yuka was related to the guy who invented gunpowder, he thought if she was he would look at her differently.

Harold imagined raising his hand.

"Yes Harold?"

"Are you at all related to the guy who invented gunpowder?"

He pictured her looking at him and then, in a gentle but somehow also stern way, saying:

"Harold, just pay attention."

In his mind he would say, "I'll pay attention but I was wondering if over Christmas vacation I could come over to your house and you could make believe you're the Empress of China and I'm the guy who just invented gunpowder and you wanted to reward me.

"How would you feel about that?"

Harold loved the birds in his head and Elizabeth and Ms. Yuka once in a while.

Sometimes he imagined he was shipwrecked with Elizabeth and Ms. Yuka on an island that had hundreds of parrots and no other kinds of birds.

The 3 of them would live in 2 different huts.

All the parrots spoke different languages and they were in groups of two so each parrot had another parrot to talk to.

This led to him imagining quietly making little parrot noises to himself just for his own amusement.

Then he thought of Pamela Clancy, who sat right beside him to his left, and what if she looked over and saw him making the little parrot noises.

This seemed so insane and funny to him that he almost peed his pants.

Then he thought that sometimes you see statues of little boys peeing into fountains but you never see statues of little girls squatting down peeing into fountains, he wondered why is that? It could be done if they wanted.

The boy wished he could have been at the meeting where that was decided.

One winter Harold was outside with his sister and she tried to pee her name in the snow and broke her ankle.

He began to pray, even though he wasn't sure if there was a God, for some kind of bird to fly through the middle of his head to stop all this madness.

A strange sociopath parakeet drifted through the rectangle causing him to put his head down on his desk and fall asleep.

Harold was asleep for about a minute but he had a three and a half hour dream. He thought how can that be?

He assumed that dream time must be different than awake time.

The dream Harold had was about a guy who was trying to train a turtle to be a contortionist.

Harold had some unusual interests:

He loved stencils and the word *stencil* and what it meant and he thought that if he ever had a little girl he might name her Stencilina.

"Hello, I'd like you to meet my daughter Stencilina."

Maybe there could be twins: Stencilina and Stencileenia.

They would be so identical that the only way you could tell them apart was if you wrote their names down.

Then another bird flew through the middle of Harold's head that made him think that all twins were live stencils.

The boy loved interesting words. Words that had a nice sound combined with what they meant.

Stencil stencil stencil.

In some cases it stunned Harold how things could change.

Like the horrible dictators and mass murderers or murderers in general.

How they were once little babies looking up into someone's eyes.

How can this be? How?

Harold was a wondering machine.

God made Harold specifically to wonder. If there was a God.

Whenever he heard about somebody's parents getting divorced he liked to imagine the girl walking down the aisle and then the priest saying:

"You may now kiss the bride."

And then later there they are sitting at tables on opposite sides of the courtroom all serious and sad and angry.

Harold thought wouldn't it be weird if every time the guy wanted to kiss his wife the priest had to be there and say:

"You may now kiss the bride."

And then later after the whole thing went bad the priest would say:

"You may now divorce the bride."

Harold was fascinated by divorce proceedings and outcomes.

A very beautiful dark blue bird with black eyes and a beak that looked like it had a small smile flew through the rectangle.

Harold thought that say for instance a husband got up one morning and drove to the nearest airport and didn't tell his wife he was doing this and then he got on a plane and flew three and a half hours to another city and then he rented a car and drove two hours out to a small town and his wife didn't know anything about this and there was a bank in this town and then he went in to rob the bank and then during the robbery tragically one of the security guards was killed and he was arrested and then he was sentenced to 25 years to life in prison and the wife didn't know anything about this plan, she didn't contribute to the plan, she didn't help organize the plan, she had nothing to do with it, the husband thought of this and did all of it completely on his own, and now he's going to do 25 years to life in prison, was she going to do half?

One time in class Steven Srike raised his hand and asked Ms. Yuka if mass murder meant that all murders took place in Massachusetts and Harold remembered that the way Ms. Yuka told him this was not what it meant was so kind and gentle and loving that he wanted to hug her.

Harold's childhood was taking place in Massachusetts.

A very small red and yellow beaked bird flew through the rectangle in Harold's head and he wondered what was written on the other side of the blackboard.

The blackboard was green. Yes it was. This was another piece of knowledge going into his head which was that the world was nuts and even the people in charge were very wrong on things even though they were adults.

He wanted to raise his hand and ask Ms. Yuka what color the blackboards were in China but he didn't because he just wasn't in the mood.

Harold raised his hand.

"Yes, Harold?"

"Ms. Yuka, do you happen to know what's written on the other side of the blackboard?"

"Excuse me?"

"Nothing."

Harold asked it quietly on purpose so she couldn't understand just to amuse himself.

Harold raised his hand.

"Yes Harold?"

"Ms. Yuka, did you know that rickshaws were in Japan before they were in China where their popularity really took off at the turn of the century?"

"Excuse me Harold?"

"Nothing."

Ms. Yuka asked the class who knew where Miami was and Harold didn't know why because he was busy with his own mind and his own life and part of him thought that being asked a question by Ms. Yuka or anyone really was an invasion of privacy.

In fact he remembered when his grandfather told him that he considered being alive an invasion of privacy.

He was in and out of paying attention like someone who was away and occasionally came by to pick up their mail.

It became a routine for Harold that whenever Ms. Yuka said:

"May I have your attention."

Under his breath he would say:

"Get your own attention."

He did of course know exactly where Miami was because of the black globe and because his family had gone to Florida one summer on vacation.

They went in the summer because it was cheaper.

Harold remembered driving by a billboard that was advertising glass bottom boats and just then a bird flew through the rectangle in his head and he thought wouldn't it be great if he had a pair of glass bottom shoes that he could wear on the glass bottom boat with no socks on so that if the fish looked up they could for the first time in their lives see bare feet that weren't in the water.

One of Harold's hobbies was to try to see the world through the eyes of other people or animals.

He learned to do this by doing the opposite of what his mother did.

Elizabeth raised her hand.

"Yes Elizabeth?"

"It's in Florida. You drive through it when you go to the Florida Keys which is where Ernest Hemingway used to live."

"Yes, very good, Elizabeth."

Harold raised his hand.

"Yes, Harold."

"Nothing."

He raised his hand again.

"Do you have a question, Harold? When you raise your hand you're supposed to have a question."

"What was the name of that tribe of Indians you were talking about a few months ago that had two names?"

"That was the Lakota and the white man called them Sioux. Why do you ask?"

"Just curious."

He thought the Lakota was the most interesting thing Ms. Yuka had ever talked about.

Ms. Yuka was a stunningly average looking woman.

She was about between 28 and 32ish years old, 5' 8" tall. With a build that was about 15% slimmer than medium.

She wore a black skirt that went to just above her knees. And usually some kind of shirt/blouse type thing. Always black flat heeled shoes.

Dark dark brown eyes that showed her mostly happy very alive spirit.

Shoulder-length black hair that she wore in different female type arrangements.

Ms. Yuka loved being an elementary school teacher. The class would never ever know how much.

She partially grew up in Chengde China, which is 111 miles from Beijing.

At the age of 8 her family moved to South Dakota then to New England.

Once Ms. Yuka gave the class the assignment to write their autobiographies right then, in one hour. Her mistake was saying there was no wrong way of doing it.

Harold wrote: *Born and now 7. The end.*

100% direct, accurate, true.

Harold loved living in the circus in his head. He saw his mind as a soup made up of a mixture of what was on the inside of his head and what was on the outside of his head.

He considered himself a brain chef.

This is how Harold saw what was happening inside his head.

He felt the way his mind worked was that there were thousands and thousands and thousands of tiny birds in his head and each bird represented a single thought.

There was also a little very very small rectangle in the middle of his brain. Like an empty window frame or an empty picture frame.

The birds were much smaller than the frame.

They were flying all around randomly in his mind which was like an indoor sky.

When one of these birds flew through the rectangle whatever thought that bird represented that's what Harold would think about.

That's why it seemed like he would jump from subject to subject. It was because of the birds and the rectangle.

For instance a bird that represented lifeboats once flew through the rectangle.

So Harold was now thinking about lifeboats which led to this:

There were 25 kids in the class—what if they were on a ship that was sinking?

He figured that a lifeboat could only take 20 people so which 5 kids wouldn't get on?

Slowly he looked around the room trying to imagine who would be the lucky ones.

This reminded him of the tragedy of the *Titanic*. Not nearly enough lifeboats.

And then the fact that the sinking of the ship, April 15, 1912, knocked the opening of Fenway Park that same week out of the headlines.

Which caused him to wonder how Carl Yastrzemski would do next season.

That bird started a tangent festival in Harold's head.

A tangent festival.

Who would ever have known that the subject of lifeboats would lead to the left fielder for the Boston Red Sox.

God was hilarious. If there was a God.

A very black bird with orange wing tips flew into the rectangle and then circled within it a couple of times and then flew out bringing this thought about lifeboats:

Why don't any of the lifeboats in the history of the world have sails? They would be "sail lifeboats" and they could just sail all the way to safety, even thousands of miles.

Harold also had thoughts on his own that were not brought by the birds.

For instance he felt there should be lifeguard chairs everywhere because people needed to be saved more places than just in the water.

As far as the class and a lifeboat, they always say:

"Women and children first," so that would mean everyone.

Harold resented being a child other than if he was on a ship that was sinking.

He didn't like the label of being a kid and all that people thought it meant. What people assume someone knows or doesn't know pissed him off.

A red bird with a green head and yellow tipped wings sped through the rectangle bringing this thought:

"A kid knew more by knowing less."

Since he had less information in his head maybe he could see the overall picture better, bigger without being blocked by lots of facts.

Like looking at a photograph of the earth taken from outer space. Taken by the men on the Apollo.

Plus of all the wars in the history of the world none of them were started or caused by children.

This was a major factor overlooked by the general population and proved that the adults were the real idiots.

All the crimes against humanity: adults.

So to have to raise his hand to get permission to go take a leak or ask a question infuriated him.

Harold wondered how old you had to be to realize that you were crazy. This was not related to what he just expressed.

He felt strongly that it would be harder to figure out if a child was crazy as opposed to a grown-up.

In fact children have a "built in craziness" that automatically comes with the child.

Like a new car with a great stereo.

Harold was hoping Elizabeth would turn around for some reason so he could see her face.

She was a pretty girl. Blue eyes blonde hair. A calm sparkleness to her.

Harold thought what does that mean?

The structure of her face when his eyes see it tells his brain that yes, "we" like this, "we" like how this looks, and therefore "we" would like to see it again and again and "we" would like to talk to this person and "we" would like to spend time with this person.

He concluded that this makes no sense. He thought "we" because Harold considered himself plural. He had for several years now.

The way he saw it was that if this was the 1500s Elizabeth would be a princess and he would be one of the 10,000 peasants and his job would be to clean the moat around the castle where she lived and this started to anger him because he didn't like that job and just then Ms. Yuka said:

"Who knows how far the earth is from the sun?"

Harold imagined yelling:

"Look it up!"

But he didn't, instead under his breath he said:

"93 million miles. It takes 8 minutes for the light to travel that distance."

He didn't want to say the answer to Ms. Yuka because although he was fond of her he wanted to remain with very little contact between them because he knew even at 7 years old that women were magical creatures and like all magic creatures they could kill you without even touching you.

Even Elizabeth? Could Elizabeth do this too? How could that be?

But he thought yes, it is true.

Even an angel could beat someone to death with their wings. Each day has darkness and light.

Out the window there was a street about 100' away and going by slowly was a hearse followed by cars that were in the funeral procession that had their lights on.

He began counting the cars.

Harold remembered how when he first saw cars that were following a hearse and they had their lights on his father told him the lights were a symbol so people would know that those cars were in the funeral procession then a few nights later he was outside his house going to look up at the stars and he saw all these cars driving by in both directions and they all had their lights on and for a second he couldn't believe how many people had died then he realized the lights were on because it was nighttime then he wondered if there ever was a funeral at night and then would the cars in that procession all have to have their high beams on to make sure people knew they were in the procession.

Harold began to wonder who was going to drive his hearse at his funeral. He wondered where that guy was right now or if he was even alive right now?

Maybe he was a baby right now sucking milk from his mother's breast and then he thought the next time he sees a baby breastfeeding he's going to look at him and imagine to himself "That little baby is going to grow up and drive my hearse" and then he imagined that he would want to go over and say hi to that baby but he knew that he couldn't because the mother would think he came over there just to see one of her tits and she couldn't in a million years realize why he really went over there which was to see that baby, that little baby that might someday drive his hearse.

But maybe the driver is an adult already and if he knew who it was wouldn't it be great to go for a ride with him in the hearse just to see what kind of a driver he is?

And that way when he was dead in the hearse it would be the second time he was in it and then he would already be a little bit used to it.

That made Harold wonder if there were other things you could do now to help you be used to being dead. Used to being dead.

Sleeping to Harold was a temporary version of being dead because you don't really remember being asleep when you wake up.

The only thing you might remember is a dream, if you had one, but without a dream sleeping is the absence of conscious experience.

Maybe God did this on purpose, if there is a God. Harold didn't really know for sure of course.

Like every other person who had ever been alive in the history of the world Harold really wasn't sure if there was a God.

The only thing about this fact that bothered Harold was that he didn't like to belong to groups.

He felt that some people firmly believed there was a God but just because they believed it that didn't mean they knew it.

One of the subjects Harold could answer quickly was where a certain country or city was in the world.

He was indeed an expert because his father once spray-painted a globe all black and would ask him where certain places were in the world and Harold would have to point to where he thought they would be.

His father knew the whole globe even though it was all black because he scraped a little bit of the paint off where Hiroshima was and could judge the entire earth from there because of his military experience in WWII and his basic general knowledge.

From doing this over and over Harold knew the earth well.

Harold raised his hand.

"Yes Harold?"

"Do you happen to know the history of trick questions?"

The look Ms. Yuka gave Harold said:

"I am everything and you my poor boy are nothing. You make Oliver Twist look like Rockefeller."

Then she said, "Do you have any other questions?"

"No Ms. Yuka, I do not, no further questions at this time."

He really did have another 1100 questions but decided not to ask any of them.

To him she didn't deserve his questions.

Harold kept realizing how magnificent it was and actually how way more important it was to not say things as it was to say them.

He thought that someday he would write a book that was all blank pages and the title would be:

What I Didn't Say

The birds in Harold's head kept going and going. Some would get tired and land and rest at the bottom of his head and then go up again and fly around.

They made no sound. No bird noises, that's just how it was.

One of the birds that flew through the window inside Harold's head was the thought that if someone you knew died would they take a small piece of you with them?

At first this made him nervous and seemed like a negative thing but then he thought "no," this might be a good thing in bringing a piece of you to the side of death so that when you die you would be a little bit used to it already and it wouldn't be as quite a shock.

It would be like going for a ride in your hearse ahead of time.

Maybe that's what happens and maybe God did that on purpose. If there is a God.

Not knowing if there was a God sometimes made Harold smile because he always liked mysteries and surprises.

Chapter 2

Elizabeth raised her hand and asked if she could go to the bathroom. Harold was stunned and focused because he was so taken by her.

He thought of pictures of the universe he had seen and how giant outer space was and how it reminded him of being born and then he wondered how could he be excited about this little girl walking past him in reference to the universe?

She had pretty blue eyes and blonde hair, the universe didn't. She could smile, the universe couldn't.

She wore the same worn out red shoes every day and the universe didn't even have shoes.

Harold realized a bird must have flown through the rectangle window in the center of his head that made him compare Elizabeth's shoes to the universe. That bird made him smile.

Sometimes when Harold was outside and he saw a bird fly by he would wonder what thought that bird could represent to the world?

Ms. Yuka said:

"Yes."

And the wingless angel stood up and began her tiny journey.

Harold watched her looking down at her red shoes, listening to the little squeak that the left one made with each step.

He took a huge breath to see if he could smell Elizabeth at all.

His theory was she would have some kind of sweet scent like mint or tall summer grass in the middle to late August.

Part of him wished she smelled like nail polish remover which he thought was just tremendous.

But he couldn't smell anything so he sniffed even harder and became slightly disoriented.

Looking at the wingless angel Harold firmly believed her shadow should be in color.

His grandfather once told him that shadows were bad mirrors and they both laughed.

He also told him that a man should have locks on his mirrors because it's never too good for someone to see completely how they really are.

Harold thought how weird and strange it must be to be a girl.

He was glad he wasn't one because he didn't think he would be able to do that.

Or he wouldn't want to do that.

It's probably good that you are what you are and that's it.

You don't get to be both then choose after testing them out.

This was in the 1960s not like many many years later when it would become like going through a sexual identity salad bar.

Plus being a girl and then someday maybe having a baby growing inside of you horrified Harold.

What could possibly be stranger than that?

An exponential invasion of privacy.

As he got older he saw that being a guy was 100 times easier than being a woman.

In fact quite often he would mention it in his prayers in the section of being very thankful for what he has.

Yes, sometimes he prayed even though he wasn't sure there was a God.

If it turned out there was no God it didn't matter because then he could see his prayers as little poems.

Later when Harold was in college he would jokingly tell his girlfriends:

"You should have gotten the no maintenance genitals."

Harold was Catholic. Or he was told he was Catholic.

Just like he was told what day he was born and told what his name was.

Told, told, told.

That's all there is to it. That's it. Have a good life.

To Harold one of the main problems about being alive was the way the human mind worked because he thought it was really way out of anyone's control. He didn't mean the rectangle.

You're a baby, a toddler, a child.

Then they put a funnel into the top of your brand new very susceptible impressionable brain and just pour whatever they want into it.

The parents, society, civilization.

Sometimes they even take a shit right into the funnel.

Harold felt that everyone was like a snowblower or a lawn mower or any other machine.

Built by someone else using the available elements.

With this assembly comes the illusion of deciding what you're doing and why.

To Harold girls were like aliens that happened to be the closest species to boys on the earth.

That's why they knew each other because they were close, just close.

Meaning they were closer than giraffes or leopards or other animals.

That's why men married women instead of hyenas or turtles.

Harold imagined himself being married to a turtle and almost spit on the back of Louise Cornman's head.

Introducing her to people:

"This is my wife Darcy, be careful don't step on her.

"Darcy, this is Bob Foley from the circus.

"Don't worry I already told him we're not interested."

The way he figured it Elizabeth should be walking back into the class in less than a minute.

And he was correct, the door in the back of the class opened and Elizabeth walked between the rows of desks toward her seat and when she got right next to him he imagined saying to her:

"I want to marry you."

"What?"

"I want to go to the prom with you."

"What?"

"I'm tired of you being a stranger."

Ms. Yuka kindly said:

"Elizabeth, please sit down."

And she did.

Harold thought Elizabeth's shoulder length blonde hair would be very beautiful in braids but then he changed his mind.

He changed it because he had an uncle he never met who was killed in WWII by the Nazis two weeks before the war ended.

And that's how lots of the Nazi girls wore their hair. They were blonde too. Blonde with pretty braids.

Nazi girls.

Just then two birds flew through the window inside Harold's head.

One brought the idea wouldn't it be great if the guy who invented puppets had a fistfight with the guy who invented marionettes and they fought until one was unconscious.

The other bird represented the thought that people who speak more than one language might be crazy.

Elizabeth was a little girl with the mind of a little girl who was living on the earth in the mid-1960s sitting 3 seats up from him with her pretty eyes.

Harold had small dark eyes and as his father used to say:

"Looked like two piss holes in the snow."

He wondered why he imagined asking her those questions when she walked by?

Was it because of his built-in craziness?

He didn't wonder if there was something wrong with him because he figured at 7 years old the part of his brain that was in charge of such things was not open for business yet.

Just then Harold raised his hand.

"Yes Harold?"

This was a ridiculous question he was asking for his own amusement just to see how she would answer.

"Ms. Yuka, when you were little growing up in China did you used to think that if you dug a very very deep hole all the way through the earth you would come out the other side and be somewhere in the United States?"

"No Harold, we weren't that stupid."

Harold was tired. He was tired of thinking and tired of his mind and tired of wondering about everything and he turned and looked out the window up toward the top of a tall maple tree in the distance and saw a big hawk just floating along like in slow motion just dancing, bouncing along in the breeze which was the color of the sky and he wasn't even flapping his wings and he was alone but he wasn't lonely and Harold knew that his life in this world was a whole other thing and he couldn't imagine if that hawk was one of the birds that flew through the rectangle in his head what thought he would represent other than total wisdom and being a species that was here since the time of dinosaurs and Harold was in awe and he knew that bird had seen the Lakota and knew the Lakota when this place was theirs and Harold knew that that was what it was supposed to be like, not all this mall shit and politician assholes and commercials and worldwide small talk festivals about haircuts and white teeth and matching fucking shirts.

Harold loved the Lakota Indians and felt bad that they now lived on reservations in North and South Dakota.

A small pretty yellow and black canary, the kind that an old lady would buy in a pet store and be thrilled to have its company living alone in her house since her husband of 48 years passed away, flew through the rectangle reminding Harold his grandfather told him the following:

On his deathbed he wanted to be given the second to the last rites just to aggravate the system.

And he never had a birth certificate and to give the finger to the rules of the world one last time he wanted his birth certificate to be awarded to him posthumously.

He also wanted a recording of the ocean playing at his wake but gave no explanation why.

The man hated magicians because to him they were like politicians except they lied visually and he despised politicians.

Harold was very close to his grandfather having spent the entire summer with him when his mother was put into an insane asylum temporarily.

Also Harold was at the beginning of his life and his grandfather was near the end so they had a connection in both being near the entrance and exit of living.

Two doors side by side. Two important doors.

Harold thought that would be a good name for a book: *The Two Doors*.

His grandfather lived in a big old house on Moosehead Lake in Maine, very north, almost at the Canadian border.

The place had no phone and no electricity but his grandfather said it didn't matter because he didn't either.

Harold's mother was in the asylum for one reason and one reason only—she could not and would not stop talking.

In 1926 a pilot that was in an uncontrolled nose dive in a crazed panic pushed the yoke forward, which was exactly the wrong thing to do, but because of how fast the plane was going it caused the opposite effect it normally would have and the plane came up out of the nose dive and the pilot regained control of the aircraft.

This technique was used in future predicaments through-out aviation history.

One of the doctors at the insane asylum knew of this and in an attempt to get Harold's mother to stop talking asked her to talk even more. But it didn't work. It just did not work.

While Ms. Yuka was talking about something he wasn't listen-ing to, Harold was doing a drawing which was a version of the Last Supper from Jesus's point of view.

All the other tables and chairs in the restaurant had been pushed off to the side.

Two waiters and a waitress were standing there smoking cigarettes watching the bearded men drinking.

There was a dog asleep on the floor in front of them.

Harold had the waitress look like Brigitte Bardot, smiling and looking down at the dog.

The dog was having a dream he was in a room with Jesus, the apostles, and Brigitte Bardot.

The dog was a genius and if he had been a person would have been elected president of the United States but would have refused to take office because of integrity and a lack of arrogance.

Harold figured that 75% of the time that he was amused he amused himself. He did have some funny friends though, for instance Gerry.

Gerry was tall and skinny and funny. He was the first extrovert that Harold ever knew.

Harold realized that adults were always saying and describing how the world worked and he felt sorry for them because he knew they believed it and he knew they knew nothing and thought they knew everything which was the lowest rung on the whole ladder.

But he was happy and grateful they said all these things because that's where some amount of the amusement came from.

Harold raised his hand.

"Yes Harold?"

"Ms. Yuka, if there was no earth what do you think the moon would do with all the energy it uses now to move the tides?"

"Well Harold, I really have . . ."

Harold under his breath: "Ms. Yuka, I would love to kiss the backs of your legs while you were in line in a bank."

"Excuse me, Harold?"

"Nothing just thank you anyway."

Then he thought that was another part of the 75%.

Harold wondered who the first left-handed man was and who was the first guy that noticed the other guy was left-handed.

That conversation might have gone like this:

"Hey, Teddy, why are you doing that with your left hand?"

"Because I'm left-handed."

"Oh I didn't know that could happen. I've never seen that before."

"Well you learn something new every day."

"No you don't."

Then a possible fistfight.

Chapter 3

Harold would never lie but he realized some things were giant lies and nobody complained about them and some of them were even cherished like Fairy Tales and all Religions.

A Dutch Meerket, which is a duck with a black pointed beak native to Holland, glided gently through the rectangle in Harold's head as he looked at Ms. Yuka.

This bird brought the thought that a person's teeth are the only part of the human skeleton that you can see while the person is still alive.

They're like a skeleton preview.

Harold smiled at this new fact just delivered to him.

He wished there was a way to thank the little Dutch bird living inside his head.

He watched Ms. Yuka talking to the class and he thought of raising his hand:

"Yes Harold?"

"I just want to let you know that with that mouth full of

pearls you have it looks like you're going to leave an out-standing bone situation."

Then he thought of the envelope on his dresser that contained all his baby teeth.

He saw them differently now. As if without knowing it he'd been living near a small archeological site.

It also made him feel like he'd experienced a toy version of reincarnation. Keeping something from his previous life.

He decided when he died he wanted the baby teeth to be buried with him.

After all they were as much a part of his skeleton as his second set of teeth were.

They paved the way and they should be respected.

He loved the sound the envelope made when he shook it, like a cheap maraca.

He also thought that he would like to be buried 7' deep for more privacy.

Harold once saw a beautiful green and rust and yellow col-ored bird that looked exactly like one that he had seen inside his head a few days earlier.

The bird looked right at him then winked.

This same bird inside his head flew through the rectangle again as Harold was watching Ms. Yuka.

It caused the thought about those Russian dolls.

How there's one, then a smaller one inside that one, then a smaller one inside that one and on and on and on.

Harold now thought that's what it's like when a woman gives birth to a baby girl—on and on and on and on.

A boy doesn't fit into that situation which was fine with Harold because he had other things to do.

Like thinking back how when he was in Maine his grandfather kiddingly told him that all the chairs around the dining room table had been used by different people who had hung themselves.

He would say:

"Harold, would you like to sit in Mr. Simpson's chair or Hanna Sue's?

"Sit wherever you like Harold, sit wherever you like. Just don't stand on any of the chairs!"

He would then cackle madly and throw a spoon against the window.

Sometimes they would make up stories about why the people did it.

"Harold, it's a shame that Mr. Simpson would do such a thing just because he didn't know what time it was."

"Yes Pa, it is, it's a crying shame."

"If you ever want to know what time it is what are you going to do?"

"Pa, if I ever want to know what time it is I'll ask someone. Or I'll just kill myself."

Both of them:

"Hahahahaha!!!"

He told Harold that there's way more people who had lived and died than were alive right now, so being alive was a rare thing and should be appreciated while it was happening.

He said being alive is a minority.

He knew Harold wouldn't know what he meant for a very very long time but that was ok.

He smiled at Harold and said:

"I'm glad we're alive at the same time. That's a pretty lucky thing."

Harold thought it was too bad he and his grandfather weren't old men at the same time or young boys at the same time.

Then he thought that was just asking for too much.

The old man told his little grandson that 112 billion people had already lived and died. They were here and are now gone.

"Your table is ready."

He said there are 15 dead people for every person living.

Years later as a college student Harold looked up these numbers and verified they were accurate.

He was never aware of how his grandfather knew this.

Harold resented that when you were born determined what time in history you lived—

He felt that birth had an undeserved claim to time. Although he understood the logic.

From another angle he looked at many things.

A hummingbird a third larger than normal flew through the rectangle.

Harold realized that everyone he knew or was related to or had seen or was in the class with right now including Ms. Yuka all knew each other because they were all accidentally born around the same time.

He was overwhelmed with the flukiness of this and begged that another bird bringing any other subject would fly through the rectangle and just then Ms. Yuka started talking in Chinese and Harold wasn't sure why because he wasn't paying attention but at least now he was thinking about something else and he raised his hand and Ms. Yuka, in English, said:

"Yes Harold?"

"Thank you."

"Yes, that's correct, very good, Harold. I didn't think you were listening."

He looked to his left, past the two rows of students, out the window to see if there was a bird out there.

Sometimes just looking out the window was like going on a little adventure from the classroom.

He loved birds so very much and until he was about 4 years old he thought that all birds knew each other.

How he found out they didn't was he was sitting on Santa Claus's lap and Santa asked him what he wanted for Christmas and Harold told him that he wanted all lies to be true then Harold asked him if all birds knew each other and Santa said no.

He didn't see any birds.

But he noticed the very tall maple trees blowing back and forth in the breeze and he thought wouldn't it be great if people kept getting taller and taller the older they got like trees did and then you could be walking down the street and see a nice skinny old lady who was 90 years old who was about 35' tall and she could have a long cane made out of several bamboo poles latched together and she would be so happy because she could see such great distances and she might see Harold standing on the sidewalk looking up at her and she might slowly bend way over like a giraffe until her head was about 5½' off the ground and she could say:

"And what's your name, little boy?"

And then he could say, "My name is Harold."

And then she could say:

"Oh that's a very nice name, I used to have a bird named Harold, he was a grey cockatoo and I had him for many many years, I got him a long time ago when I was about 20' tall. Do you like birds, Harold?"

"Oh yes I love birds so much, birds are one of my favorite things about being alive, I love to see them and watch them when they fly by."

"Oh Harold, I do too! That's one of the best things about being an old lady, the bird-watching is just amazing, simply amazing, maybe someday we could go bird-watching together, wouldn't that be nice?"

"Yes."

"Well, you have a nice day Harold, my name is Betty, so nice to meet you, goodbye."

"Goodbye, Betty."

Ms. Yuka was now talking about doing a play in the class after Christmas and then maybe doing it in the school auditorium.

Rather than her choosing the play she asked the class if they knew any play they would like to do?

Or would they like to make one up?

She asked if anyone in the class had ever been to a play before?

Brenda O'Hearne, who was one of the smallest girls in the class who always sat in the front row in the middle for the yearly picture, raised her hand.

"Yes Brenda?"

"I saw *A Christmas Carol*."

"Oh and how did you like it?"

"I liked it."

"Why did you like it?"

"Because I liked the story."

"What did you like best about it?"

"Our seats."

A bird in the canary family, but not in the immediate canary family, flew through the rectangle and Harold thought they could do a play about the most famous hermit in the world.

He knew this idea could have problems, for instance how could there be more than one person in the play?

Then he thought there could be many people in it if the hermit had a press conference.

He would have it because he was the most famous hermit in the world and the irony in that tickled Harold from the inside.

He figured that it would either be very bad or fantastic, but no in-between.

He thought of raising his hand and suggesting it to Ms. Yuka but he knew she wouldn't like it and during her rejecting it she might even ask him if he would want to be the hermit and then he would wish she was underwater so she couldn't hear him and he could say:

"No Ms. Yuka, I'm already a hermit in real life so I don't need to play one onstage and if you're saying no to it anyway why are you even asking me?"

But he didn't raise his hand.

Harold didn't like musicals, they irritated him.

Except for the ones that Judy Garland was in. He was in love with Judy Garland.

He thought she was beautiful and had an amazing magical voice.

When he saw her in a movie nothing else mattered. That's it. That's just how it was.

There was one play he liked, with no singing of course, and that was *Our Town*.

He liked when the girl died and then she went under the ground and was talking to some of the people who had already died before.

The play was about that people basically miss their whole lives because they're too busy running around. He thought that was pretty amazing even though he was only 7.

Harold thought cemeteries should have a staircase where you could go down and talk to the people like in the play.

He saw the play in Maine with his grandfather at the old playhouse near the lake.

Here's an example of what Harold thought of someone's opinion.

One time in first grade everyone was supposed to be drawing a picture.

The teacher, Mrs. Walsh, was walking around the classroom looking at the creations on the children's desks. She got beside Harold's desk.

"Oh Harold, what a nice picture that is, that really is very pretty and very interesting."

Harold wished that Mrs. Walsh was underwater so he could have said:

"How dare you judge me."

Two small birds that obviously knew each other flew through the rectangle extremely fast with the tips of their wings almost touching.

They were so close they brought one thought which was another play called *The Reverse Birthday*.

This revolved around the fact that every year a person is alive they pass the date that they're going to die but they don't know it.

So Harold thought that in the play there could be a magic mirror that you hold up to your birthday date and it shows the date that you die.

Then people would have two parties a year to celebrate rather than just one.

The second party would be to celebrate that you had a life to live.

Harold wondered that every year on the date you're going to die something happens that you're not aware of because you don't know what the date is.

Like maybe something goes wrong every year on that date. Or maybe something fantastic or fun or very enjoyable happens on that date but nobody ever connects it because they don't know.

He didn't bother raising his hand because he knew she wouldn't like that one either.

She would want something that had paper trees in it.

Paper trees hahaha.

Harold was pissed off that Ms. Yuka was asking the class to suggest or make up a play.

He thought it was like she was asking the class to come up with a test and then take it.

What if he raised his hand and said:

"Yeah while you're at it why don't you have clocks invent time and have clouds control the wind?

"And by the way why do I have to raise my hand every time I want to say something?

"What is this bullshit? This only happens in school.

"You're supposed to be preparing us for the world and instead you're giving us timid lessons.

"Like paint-by-number books and ridiculous coloring books.

"Bells going off to do this and that.

"How about teaching us something that doesn't remove our thinking?

"Is this a school or a lobotomy factory?"

But Harold didn't say anything and just sat quietly beside the warm fireplace inside his head and thought of WWII B-17 bombers dropping sweaters instead of bombs.

He thought of this for no reason, no reason at all.

It could have been a bird.

Or the huge Flying Fortress built by Boeing could be dropping straitjackets slowly floating down on parachutes.

And all the insane people, which includes everybody, would run out into the open fields somehow in slow motion to keep pace with the parachutes, running and running and running and before they put them on everybody could sit on a giant blanket and have a great big picnic, drinking wine laughing and laughing and then put on their straitjackets and go even further insane.

When Harold's mother was a resident of the asylum he wondered if the place had an auditorium and if so what kind of play they would try to put on?

One thing he knew for sure was that his mother couldn't be in it because then no one else would get to talk.

Once when Harold was at the asylum building a bird got caught in the revolving door.

He turned the door so the open part faced the lobby and the bird flew in.

The boy was fascinated by how a bird acted when he was trapped inside a building.

How they flew around desperately trying to solve the problem and figure the way out back into the sky.

Sometimes that's how Harold felt in general.

In the lobby the bird kept banging into the glass of an office door and Harold thought that would be a perfect place to have a gift shop if the insane asylum was going to have one.

You walk in and the lady behind the counter says:

"Can I help you?"

"Oh I'm just browsing."

Harold thought that could also be the name of his autobiography—

Just Browsing

"Excuse me, how much are these straitjacket key chains?

"Do these pop-up nervous breakdown books come in hardcover?

"How much are the make believe hallucinations and are they childproof?"

He thought his autobiography could be a combination hardcover and paperback in one book at the same time and if there was ever a place to sell a book like that it would be in this gift shop.

However he had no desire to write one.

The name of the asylum was:

Gi Gi's Place.

Harold had walked slowly over to the bird in the lobby and quickly grabbed it in his hands then went out through the revolving door and threw him up into the sky.

An old woman, a resident of the asylum, was sitting there on a bench and saw this.

"Excuse me young man, do you have an eagle I could have?"

"No I'm sorry ma'am, they're all on vacation in Spain."

Chapter 4

One time in first grade Harold raised his hand and asked Mrs. Walsh if he could go to the bathroom and she said yes.

He didn't get up or move or anything, Mrs. Walsh was just looking at him.

"I don't have to go I just wanted to know if I could go."

There were many birds inside Harold's head that made him think of his grandfather and his house on the lake.

A huge wooden structure built a little after the turn of the century.

The sides were weathered shingles brown and almost black. The trim was wood painted green.

It had an elevator that worked by pulling a rope that was connected to weights and pulleys.

You could go from the small room at the very top down past the 3rd and 2nd floors that both had bedrooms then past the main floor and then into the dirt floor cellar at the very bottom where they kept the rowboats.

Harold tried to imagine what it would be like if he and Elizabeth and his grandfather were ever on that elevator together.

His grandfather might ask:

"Elizabeth, what would you say to me if you were an old lady and I was a little boy?"

"I would say you look pretty good for an old man."

"Oh that's interesting, it's because I drink a lot of water."

Even though this never happened Harold would consider it an artificial memory.

He learned that from his grandfather too.

He told Harold there were many more things in his head that never happened than were actually happening because that's just how the brain worked.

He said the brain was way too powerful to just focus on what was really happening.

It was like having a jet engine on a flyswatter.

For instance:

Harold wondered if bird angels would have four wings.

He thought of asking Ms. Yuka but he didn't because, like most adults, he didn't think she could think beyond reality.

If he did ask her this is how it may have gone—

"Ms. Yuka, do you think that bird angels would have four wings?"

Blank controlled firm look two steps below a stare.

"Harold, please pay attention."

Then he would wish she was underwater so he could say:

"I am paying attention, I'm paying attention to what I'm

thinking about not what you want me to be paying attention to—if you want to look at it from a legal point of view."

Another random thought by the overactive mind:

"Why would there ever be a needle in a haystack in the first place?"

And imagine saying to someone:

"So exactly when did you lose track of time?"

The windows of the large living room faced the lake about 100' away.

Harold and his grandfather had many conversations in this room about many subjects. They were recorded in his brand new brain.

He told him there can be many truths to the same subject. Like a bicycle wheel.

If the hub of a wheel was the subject, the spokes leading to it would be different perspectives.

All of them true even if different.

He said this was a view of the world that the Lakota had. In their analogy there was a circle for the sun and then many rays coming out from it.

In 1941 he worked as a surveyor building the Ellsworth Air Force base in Rapid City, South Dakota.

The construction began right after Pearl Harbor. Some Lakota worked on it with him and he became great friends with one of them.

His name was Own Time.

Meaning you're in your own time. Not owning time. The idea of owning anything was not in the world of the Lakota.

Harold's grandfather told him his Lakota name could be Boy of Many Nows.

Right outside a porch ran the length of the house.

A couple of rocking chairs painted green were casually sitting out there.

Like they were having a quiet meeting and would stop talking when people came near.

Once his grandfather was in the living room walking toward the fireplace and there was a cricket on the floor in front of him, he said excuse me and walked around him.

On the many many walls in the huge house there were hooks to hold paintings.

Approximately 35 total counting all 3 floors.

There was only 1 painting.

Every few days or weeks or whenever he felt like it his grandfather would move the painting to another hook. Always nowhere near the one it was just on.

It was a painting of an anchor.

One of the those huge old ones with the two pointed ends.

All rusty, it was on land with one of the hooks on the grassy ground and the other one vertical.

With the large 8' bar going on an angle to the ground.

As you looked at it from the side it was triangle-shaped.

But unlike most triangles, if this triangle was not handled correctly it could kill 15 people.

A kind of sissy bird that was turquoise with a little bit of green on its wings flew through the rectangle reminding Harold how in his neighborhood there was no one else with his name.

Then on his first day of first grade he saw that there were a couple of other boys also named Harold.

He didn't even know that could happen and was very disturbed by this.

On the bus ride home he thought about it in a deep trance.

When he finally got to his house he told his mother. He was obviously very upset.

She said, "Get away from me. Just get away from me."

His mother was very moody and Harold never knew what was going to happen.

She exuded tension.

Harold once thought of naming the birds in his head but changed his mind because there were just too many of them.

He even thought that there might be more birds on the inside of his head than on the outside of his head.

He wondered if the birds inside his head were aware of the birds on the outside of his head.

And could they communicate with each other?

When Harold spent the summer with his grandfather they wanted to see the July 4 fireworks which were on the other side of the lake.

The best place to see them without actually going all the way across the lake was up on the high hill where the cemetery was.

It was about a 20-minute walk from the house on a dirt road through the woods and was one of the those little cemeteries that had people buried there as far back as the 1700s.

The two of them stood there watching.

With a sweep of his hand the old man motioned from the headstones up toward the sky in the distance, saying:

"Look Harold, it's as if the beautiful fireworks are a celebration of the lives these people lived."

Harold looked at the exploding colors, taking in what the old man had just said. Yes, a celebration.

He imagined that if during WWII the bombs exploded presenting this glorious scene of the sky being painted, the soldiers from both sides would stop fighting and just watch.

They would sit down sharing lots of wine and sandwiches. Then when given the order to continue fighting they would say:

"Fuck you we're done."

An innocent, completely logical perspective. That would never happen because that's how man is.

The people shooting and killing each other are never the people who decided there should be a war. Never.

It's always old people sitting in nicely furnished offices.

They should be shot in these offices = no more wars.

A stunning young cardinal sped confidently through the rectangle and looked Harold in the eye from the back of his eye.

This bird brought Harold the thought that wouldn't it be great if he had a big house and in the many different rooms he could have Elizabeth at different ages.

In one room she could be 3 and another 7 and another 15 and another 23 another 35 another 51 and then another 85.

Then he could go around to the different rooms and visit her at the different ages and have little conversations and joke around and play games and she would know him even though he was still just 7 years old. What better way to get to know a girl?

Then her Lakota name could be Girl of Many Nows and it would have a whole other meaning than his Lakota name.

Since she was 7 right now when he went to visit her in that room it would be kind of funny because he would have just seen her in class that day.

She might say to him:

"Harold, when you go to see me when I'm 85, tell me I said hi and ask me how I am."

"Ok I will."

And when he saw Elizabeth when she's 85 she might say to him:

"When you go see me when I'm 7, tell me that I know you can't really know this but being a little girl is so special and I will always remember where you are in time as one of my favorite times but I won't remember a lot of the details but it doesn't matter just enjoy it all. Please remember to have a lot of fun."

And 7 year old Elizabeth's response to this might be:
"Did she send me any treats?"

Unexpectedly a fistfight breaks out in the hallway of the house between 51 year old Elizabeth and 23 year old Elizabeth about birth control and gambling.

The 35 year old tries to break it up, bumps her head, and passes out halfway in the bathroom.

The 3 year old Elizabeth is standing in the doorway to her bedroom seeing all this and starts crying.

The 7 year old Elizabeth and 85 year old Elizabeth are in their rooms in a deep sleep coincidentally having the same dream about Neil Armstrong. In the dream he reveals to his wife that he's afraid of the dark.

This is the second time having this dream for 7 year old Elizabeth and the nineteenth time for 85 year old Elizabeth.

Harold looked at the clock that was high up on the wall to his right and it said it was 11:30. The hour and the minute hands were black and the second hand was red.

An arrogant seagull with a light smell of salt bourbon glided through the rectangle and Harold imagined the meeting that the men had to discuss and decide the color of these hands.

One guy didn't give a shit and agreed to anything because he wanted to get home to his new wife who looked almost exactly like Lauren Bacall except she was in color.

His dilemma was that he thought Lauren Bacall looked much better in black and white.

But how the hell was he going to get his new wife into black and white?

She would have to be on film because even the real Lauren Bacall was in color really.

But he couldn't be married to someone on film and then he started to panic because he had questioned marrying her anyway and the reason he really married her in the first place was because she looked so much like the famous actress and now he realized he'd made a huge mistake and he just felt so stupid.

And what if he told her that even though they had only been married three weeks he wanted a divorce.

Her response:

"But why? Why, I don't understand?"

"Because you're in color and I just can't take it anymore, I'm sorry."

The order of the invention of color film and black-and-white film amused Harold.

He felt that color should have come first because that's how things really are and black-and-white should have come second because that's an abstraction, which seems more complicated.

Rembrandt came before Salvador Dalí. Harold's favorite painters.

Of course in order to feel this way he had to put the technological reality off to the side.

There was a huge amount of information on many subjects put off to the side. Huge.

He liked to imagine that the guy who invented color film and the guy who invented black-and-white film invented them at the same time.

He imagined they were friends and lived across the street from each other.

They decided to arm wrestle to see which one would come out first and the color guy lost.

Harold was fascinated about how babies were made. Not the actual sex act.

Meaning how easy and simple it was and how any two jerks could do it.

Apparently God wanted it that way, if there was a God.

As long as more babies kept coming and for what reason Harold did not know.

Of the thousands and thousands of birds that flew through the rectangle in his head, not one of them ever answered this question.

To Harold the human body was the most complicated machine in the world by far.

It was a machine made out of meat that grew completely on its own.

He saw people who had made children and he knew they couldn't change the battery in a car or build a fence or would take 40 minutes to untangle a set of Christmas tree lights.

He knew it was easier to make a baby than it was to make a cake.

It made absolutely no sense to him.

He also thought it was a good thing that the baby grew totally correctly without any contributing thought whatsoever by the mother, except for eating and sleeping.

Because if it was not that way he knew that some pregnant women would be flipping through a magazine and you might hear them say, "Oh my God, I forgot to make the baby's head!!!"

Or

"Wait a minute, did I give the baby both conscious and subconscious parts to the brain? I can't remember because I was talking to Judy on the phone about a sale on curtains."

Even the entire Apollo space program that brought men to the moon and back was not as complicated as how the human brain controlled the human eyeball.

The Apollo took thousands of people years and years to build. It did not build itself on its own after a three-minute act.

It was built by people who grew inside their mothers automatically.

Two rare Quicksandpipers flew through the rectangle.

Harold had seen regular sandpipers many times on the beach in Maine, walking around real fast, back and forth back and forth, like they were looking for a lost contact lens.

The first bird represented the thought that a rowboat is the only form of transportation where you are not facing the direction you're going, if of course you are rowing the boat.

Harold thought this could be good for people who are obsessed with the past and afraid of the future.

Maybe this was how psychiatry was invented.

Some guy was sitting at the end of the boat and his friend was rowing and talking on and on and the guy not rowing very occasionally said something like

"Yes, go on."

The rower was very very happy to have someone so focused on what he was saying and was such a great listener.

Also it was really helping him get an insightful perspective on his life and he was so grateful for this situation.

Suddenly the listening guy realized:

"Oh my God, I just thought of an absolutely ridiculous way to make money and call it a career."

The other sandpiper represented to Harold the thought that

"I guess animals are into bestiality."

When Ms. Yuka began teaching the class in September she said she was happy to meet everyone and hoped they would have fun learning throughout the year.

Harold felt that what she said was sincere and there was no reason to think she was lying.

He figured she was what he would plead if he was ever in court on trial, which was:

"I am guilty of being innocent."

She could also be very open-minded.

For instance she did not question or balk when he decided to do finger paints while wearing mittens.

This resulted in a very abstract painting that looked like several black horses arguing.

During one of the art periods Harold wanted to raise his hand and ask:

"Ms. Yuka, where would all the paintings be if walls were never invented?"

But he didn't because of a gut feeling he had.

Harold also felt that all art is modern art at some point.

As he decided not to ask her this a Verreaux's eagle-owl, which is widespread in sub-Saharan Africa and is the largest owl on the continent, glided through the rectangle causing Harold to wonder if anyone had ever had a nightmare about a herd of revengeful piñatas returning to eat and club children with sticks.

The tradition of a piñata fascinated Harold in that the parents never really made it clear that smashing this thing hanging on a rope containing candy and presents was a very unique situation.

This was the only time doing something like this made sense and was all right to do.

When his cousin Tippy was about 4 years old he was at a carnival and when he wasn't being watched for about 12 seconds he tried to crack open a merry-go-round horse with a rake handle he found on the ground, trying to get the presents that were surely hidden inside.

With a swing like Red Sox right fielder Tony Conigliaro, he hit the first horse that came around, which was light green with a yellow mane and tail, carrying a soon to be traumatized cute little girl with black braids and a nice pink dress she had on for her 3rd birthday.

She peed all over herself and the artificial horse having just drank a huge lemonade.

The combination sound of smashing the horse and the screaming little girl caused a small flock of birds that were resting on a nearby tree to exit immediately into the sky.

Two quick turns, left then right until they were out of sight.

A move Harold would have very much enjoyed to watch had he been there.

Harold liked it when Ms. Yuka was a little bit confused because she just looked kind of adorable even though she was around 30 which to Harold was about 100.

He remembered that look one time in particular when the class was talking about siblings and he told her that he was one of four only children.

When he spoke there was a slight alteration in his speech because he had two fireballs in his mouth, both on the right side.

Ms. Yuka didn't notice that but she responded by saying:

"Harold, what you just said is impossible."

"Yes but that doesn't mean it isn't true."

"Excuse me?"

Just then Karen Mitrano threw up on her desk.

While Ms. Yuka was helping her Harold said under his breath:

"My grandfather told me that in the world of the Lakota there can be many truths to the same subject.

"Although I have a sister I am still just one and so is she.

"Ms. Yuka, a shadow is also something even though it has no weight and can't be picked up, like the clouds and the light from the sun.

"Sometimes it is better to listen than to speak, maybe someday you will learn this."

He said this like Humphrey Bogart would say it.

He wondered if Humphrey Bogart liked fireballs.

A small yellow bird that looked like he was wearing a black vest that an Italian waiter would wear in the 1940s and had a look in his eyes like he was running late flew through the rectangle and Harold remembered he had a piece of driftwood about half the size of a rolling pin in the top drawer of his bureau.

He thought that maybe he should carve it into a little soldier and give it to Elizabeth for Christmas.

Even though he knew a girl wouldn't want a wooden soldier, which would be perfect because it would show he liked her but wouldn't show how much.

Because he was aware, even at his age, that if she knew how much he really liked her she would be in charge and his life would be ruined.

One day Harold's mother accidentally filled his lunch thermos with red wine instead of grape juice and then after everyone ate it was time for show-and-tell.

The pretty Margrette Alden with long black hair went up first and demonstrated how to knit a few stitches which was something her grandmother recently taught her.

Robert Zapollo brought his hamster Stanley to the front of the class in a cage and talked about his nervous behavior.

"Ok Harold you can be next."

He pushed himself up like he weighed 200 pounds, walked and swayed to the front of the class as if he was imitating John Wayne. He was smashed.

Leaning against Ms. Yuka's desk he slurred and mumbled something about Margrette stabbing Stanley to death with her knitting needles.

"Harold, is there something wrong with you?"

The young boy steadied himself looking at Elizabeth looking right at him.

Then a hawk that knew Red Cloud, the great Lakota leader from the mid-1800s, glided majestically through the rectangle bringing him strength and confidence.

"No Ms. Yuka, I am just another lost boy but I will not be lost forever."

He then slowly walked back to his desk.

As he passed Elizabeth he leaned toward her and quietly said:

"Let me know how long you'll be on the earth."

Then sat down.

"Harold, you didn't show or tell anything?"

"I showed an advanced sense of privacy for someone my age."

This was very slurred and couldn't be understood. She ignored him.

Chapter 5

Soon it would be time for Christmas vacation which Harold looked forward to every year even though this was only the 3rd one.

The imagining part of the factory in his head excitedly thought that maybe he could somehow find out where Elizabeth lived and somehow be in her neighborhood and somehow be on her street one morning when it was snowing and then coincidentally bump into her.

The following is what he pictured could happen:

"Hi Elizabeth, how are you? How's the toy soldier? I know you don't like it that much which was the whole point."

"Hi Harold, how did you know where I lived?"

"I was just walking around randomly and then I was carried here by time and now I'm here."

"Thank you for the soldier."

"Would you like to walk over to the cemetery? Because it's very beautiful over there in the snow.

"I was there a few weeks ago and saw a headstone that had the name *Elizabeth* on it and we could go look at it.

"After I saw it I looked for one that said *Harold* but didn't see one, maybe we could walk around and find one."

Wearing her new light blue knit hat and red warm coat, no response.

"Elizabeth, did you ever wonder if some of the snow we see used to be part of rivers or lakes or oceans?"

"No."

"Because there's only a certain amount of water on the earth and it just keeps going around and around and up and down.

"So if we went to the cemetery the snow there might have been part of the Indian Ocean or maybe the Mediterranean Sea.

"One time I was with my grandfather and he had tears in his eyes and I said:

"'Pa, are those crying tears or tears of laughter?'

"He said:

"'I haven't decided yet.'

"Then he started laughing so I knew they weren't sad tears. Would you like to go?"

"Ok Harold."

"There's a swing hanging off a tree over in there too. It's weird to see that in the winter."

"Why would there be a swing in a cemetery?"

"Maybe there's a little kid buried there. Poor kid. Did you know the human body is made up of 98% water?

"So we're just a bunch of snowstorms walking around too."

"How far is the cemetery, Harold?"

"About a ten-minute walk. I know the way because in a

few months I'm going to have a paper route so I've already been practicing and it goes right by there almost."

They started walking.

Harold was creating another synthetic memory.

"How many people will be on your paper route?"

"There'll be about 9 in the new neighborhood they're building.

"We should go over there sometime. I love being in houses while they're being built, the different stages they're in.

"Have you spent much time in unfinished houses?"

"No, Harold."

"My house was built before I was born so I couldn't have gone in it but I bet some older kids did. I wonder who they are."

Harold talked much more in his synthetic memories than in his real ones.

"I wish we had pictures of our house under construction. I wish I knew where they got the wood and I wish I could have seen the wood while they were still trees.

"And what I really wish was that I could see some of the birds that were in those trees.

"Do you ever wish that about your house, Elizabeth?"

"No."

"Elizabeth, sometimes I think about the casket I'm going to be in the same way. I wonder where the trees are now that will be used for the wood.

"Are they little trees just starting to grow or are they big trees ready to be cut down soon or almost soon? Or have they already been cut into lumber?

"I also wonder who's the guy that's going to drive the log truck to the mill and which mill will it be? Imagine if he was friends with the hearse driver?"

He didn't mention going for a test ride in his hearse.

"And what birds will have landed on those trees. Stood on the branches and looked around and whistled to their friends and then flew away for another fun day in the sky.

"Imagine if one of those birds was standing on a fence near your yard and you looked at him and he looked at you and maybe there was some kind of extra connection in that look?

"Imagine that, Elizabeth? You know there's been so many people and so many birds over the years I bet you that has to have happened to someone somewhere.

"Imagine little bird caskets? Would you like to make some little bird caskets out of driftwood?"

"I think you're a nice person Harold, but no I don't want to make little bird caskets. Let's just keep going."

"Ok."

He knew that if this was happening in a 1940s movie he would have said:

"I'll go anywhere with a good-looking dame like you."

Harold realized that since this was a made-up situation he could have Elizabeth say and do anything he wanted like when he thought of them being shipwrecked.

There were so many things that could happen.

Actually in your real life there were so many things that could happen too.

The difference between fiction and nonfiction was doing something.

So they started walking over to the cemetery and the strange boy imagined her saying:

"Harold, I want you to know that even though we never talk in school and even though I am only 7 I am deeply and madly in love with you."

He imagined throwing snowballs at her for no reason.

They moved down the street that was extra quiet because of the snow.

As they walked along in the artificial memory Harold said:

"Elizabeth, when I was a little boy."

Then he started laughing.

"I know I'm still a little boy, I just said that to be funny. When I was about 3 my grandfather taught me to say 'when I was a little boy' just for his own amusement.

"When I was a little boy I would stay with my grandfather in Maine and he would build birdhouses and put them up in the trees near his house. I would help him.

"One of the birdhouses he built had little fire escapes on it.

"They were made out of old guitar strings painted black and looked very real.

"He did that for his own amusement too. He did so many things like that.

"Sometimes when a bird stepped on the fire escape it made the sound of one note.

"There's a little store across the lake and he knew the guy who ran it and owned it and a few days before I visited him he would go into the store and give the guy about five dollars so that when I was visiting him we could go in and quietly walk around and shoplift.

"Of course we weren't really shoplifting because he had already paid.

"But the other people in the store didn't know that.

"It was so much fun to slowly be putting 25 fireballs in my pocket or stick an unassembled kite down my pant leg and walk with a limp like a pirate.

"The building was old with dark wood floors that were crooked.

"Outside in front of the store was a big wooden Indian.

"I remember one time being down the end of an aisle and as I was stealing several rabbit's foot key chains I turned my head and noticed an old lady was watching me.

"So I put my finger up to my lips to indicate *do not tell* and then I quickly swiped my finger across my neck to indicate *or I will cut your throat.*

"I was 5 at the time and didn't realize how unique it was to threaten someone who was about 80 years older than me.

"Those were the days."

Elizabeth had no reaction or comment to this story and Harold would learn over the years that this would be a typical response to things he said to women.

"We could make snow angels while we're in the cemetery,

what a perfect place to make them, but too bad we couldn't make them in the sky in the flakes as they floated down.

"Now that would really be something. I guess birds would be the only ones to be able to do that.

"Birds making snow angels in a beautiful slow snowstorm falling in the cemetery."

"What are bird angels, Harold?"

"They are the angels of birds and they would have four wings."

Silence.

They walked along the quiet street toward the cemetery.

"Elizabeth, how old were you when you learned the names of the days of the week?"

"About 5, why?"

"I think that rather than just naming 7 days they should have named all 365.

"Whoever was in charge of that situation should have been fired. I think it shows a lack of effort and discipline and imagination."

"Well Harold, what are you considering doing about it?"

"Nothing I'm just pointing it out."

"Why don't you try to come up with the other 358 names? I could help you."

"Let me think about it."

He was losing track of the situation in his mind.

There were several layers of fake scenarios in his head getting all backed up, like when you look into the sky near a big city airport and you see the planes lined up one right after another all coming in to land except all the planes really do land.

The trouble Harold was having now was that he had too many thoughts in his head and they were never landing.

He wasn't really even talking to Elizabeth and he wasn't really walking to the cemetery in the snow and Elizabeth wasn't really urging him to finish naming every day of the year.

Then Harold thought that when you die your mind is full of thoughts that never landed.

So in temporary conclusion Harold figured that everyone's head might be full of tiny birds and the majority of them never land.

To keep from fainting right there in the class he had to say in his mind:

"Elizabeth, thank you for offering to help but I don't want to name the rest of the days of the year."

"Ok Harold."

He wondered:

"My God, if there is a God, what the hell has Ms. Yuka been talking about all this time?"

Harold had gone so far into his own head that being in the class seemed like when he turned his binoculars around and looked through them to make things look further away.

He looked around the class. He saw Gerry, he saw Brenda O'Hearne who looked like an amazing crisp drawing of herself.

He saw his friend Gary Weadick. They would remain friends the entire rest of their lives.

He saw the globe on the table near Ms. Yuka's desk and thought how odd it looked not to be spray-painted black.

Then he heard Ms. Yuka explain what perpetual motion was and why it was impossible.

He did not know why she was telling the class this.

An albino parakeet flew through the rectangle and then Harold thought that if his mother talked in her sleep that would mean she talked 24 hours a day and that would be a version of perpetual motion, but he kept this thought to himself, his best friend.

They continued down the quiet street to the next street and then turned right and went directly toward the cemetery.

They walked in silence, well not really in silence, in "not talking silence."

Both of them heard the sound of their boots crunching on the snow and the sound of cold.

It occurred to Harold that a silence when he was alone and a silence when he was with someone else were two different types.

The silence when he was with someone else could have a tension to it, like an invisible energy, at least from his side of it.

Harold thought that could be another title of his autobiography:

My Side of Silence

He thought the silence energy from people on elevators could propel an aircraft carrier for two or three days.

Of course he would never write an autobiography because he would consider it an in-house invasion of privacy.

He imagined what if there was a car that could run on the energy of the silence between two people.

For instance the silence between two people who were about to be divorced could easily take them back and forth across the United States several times.

In fact if they kept delaying the divorce the car would be going on and on and on in perpetual motion.

And here damn it was another example of perpetual motion within minutes of Ms. Yuka explaining how it's impossible.

But Harold kept it to himself, his best friend.

They walked into the cemetery through the stone walls on either side of the entrance and underneath the green wrought iron arch that held the name of the place in 8" letters which was:

GOOD MORNING

Casually they made their way on the dirt road that was underneath the snow.

You would never know it was a dirt road unless you had been there before or if they plowed it, which they wouldn't. Or if you waited for spring.

Two South African sparrows that were way off course and inside Harold's head flew through the rectangle both representing comments said to Harold by his grandfather which he told to Elizabeth.

"Elizabeth, you can't paint lines on a dirt road."

And: "Off at Ireland, Elizabeth. Off at Ireland."

"Harold, what are you talking about?"

"Those are sayings that my grandfather made up. The first one is just an observation.

"The second one means that you can never tell what decisions in your life will have giant consequences.

"He thought of it because when the *Titanic* left England it made one stop in Ireland before it went out into the Atlantic toward New York and then sank.

"Seven people just took the ship from England to Queenstown, Ireland, and then they got off."

"Was your grandfather one of those people?"

"Well, he was going to go all the way but he got off because he had a very bad case of poison ivy and he didn't want to be on that ship for a week in such a horrible condition.

"That's how later he made up the saying

" 'Off at Ireland.' "

"You mean you wouldn't be alive if your grandfather didn't get poison ivy?"

"Well not 100% correct because he might have been one of the survivors. We'll never know.

"So now whenever I get poison ivy I don't itch it, I just look at it and say thank you."

About 50' into the cemetery Harold said:

"Look."

Right there was a headstone that said:

Elizabeth R. Henderson
born June 16, 1849 died August 7, 1869

"She was only 20. What's your middle name, Elizabeth?"

"Rachel, it's my grandmother's first name."

"What do you think of seeing almost your exact name on a headstone?"

"It kind of feels like maybe I'm rehearsing to be a ghost."

Her actual last name was Harrison.

"And that's exactly when the Civil War was. You would look good in clothes from that time. With a dress like a farm girl."

"Harold, why are you talking about dead people so much?"

A rare Mojave Desert seagull glided calmly through the rectangle and caused Harold to say:

"Let's go look for a headstone that says *Harold*."

"Ok."

As they walked further into the cemetery it began to snow a little harder.

There was the rope swing hanging from a tree off to the right.

"Let's go over to the swing Harold, and let's swing on it."

First they wiped the snow off the seat with their mittens.

"You get on, Elizabeth, girls first in case there's danger."

"What?"

"Nothing."

She hopped up and held on to the ropes and Harold stepped behind her and started pushing her.

First a little bit to make sure the ropes were strong enough to hold her and then a little harder.

Since it was cold out and the ropes had some ice on them they were making creaking noises that sounded like ropes on a pirate ship in the movies when it's slowly rocking back and forth.

Elizabeth said:

"Harold, it sounds like the ropes on a pirate ship in the movies."

He thought:

"I'm falling in love with her but I'll deal with that later."

Back and forth she went on the swing.

When she was away from him her feet were over the headstone of *Annabel Johansen born 1795 died 1810*.

She was a sweet girl who helped her mother a lot with the chores around the house.

She had thick long reddish brown hair. She enjoyed sewing and in the spring and summer loved swimming in the river at the bottom of the hill with her friend Colby.

She had a crush on a farm boy at school. Her favorite time of the year was Christmas.

"Harold, do you want to have a turn on the swing?"

"No thank you. Elizabeth, did you ever drink coffee? Because I have some in a flask I brought with me."

"No I never have."

"Last summer I had it with my grandfather a few times because he loves it.

"It makes my mind go kind of funny, it makes the little circus in my head get even weirder after I drink it.

"I brought it to the cemetery because I remember my grandfather told me that when he dies when I come to visit where he's buried he wants me to pour coffee on his grave. So this is kind of a run-through.

"He said just because you're dead that shouldn't be the end of coffee."

Harold continued to push Elizabeth and then said:

"You can try it if you want to?"

"Ok."

Harold waited for the swing to stop and stepped in front of Elizabeth.

He reached into the inside pocket, took out the silver colored metal flask and handed it to Elizabeth.

Many things were happening for the first time at once, here and all over the world.

Harold imagined how the earth looked from a view from the Apollo spaceship.

And how one of the things happening down here was his 7 year old friend was drinking coffee for the first time while sitting on a swing in the cemetery as it snowed.

Harold asked her how she liked it.

"It tastes like cocoa with poison in it."

"We should start singing a song so for the rest of your life whenever you hear that song it will remind you of the first time you ever drank coffee. What would you like to sing?"

" 'The Tennessee Waltz.' "
"Ok Elizabeth."
They began to sing together:

*"I was waltzing with my darling to the Tennessee Waltz
when an old friend I happened to see. I introduced him to
my darling and as they were dancing my friend stole my
sweetheart from me."*

A few trees away sitting on a branch about 15' high an owl
watched them and listened.

For the rest of his life whenever that owl heard that song
he would think of this moment.

They passed the flask back and forth and smiled.

"Elizabeth, that's one of my grandfather's favorite songs.
Although he loves it he told me it's actually impossible."

"You mean to steal someone's girlfriend during a dance?"

"No not that, that could very possibly happen.

"He meant that the song is called 'The Tennessee Waltz' so
when he's dancing with his darling to 'The Tennessee Waltz'
and then his friend steals his darling while they were dancing
that's impossible because that's the name of the song they are
in so 'The Tennessee Waltz' actually has to be another song
which it isn't."

Elizabeth was looking at Harold with such a blank face
that her shadow had more expression.

He took a big swig of coffee and said:

"I love my grandfather," then started laughing.

He asked Elizabeth if she wanted more and she said:
"Yes please."

The owl was staring at Harold and was wondering if he had once flown through the rectangle in his head.

His big eyes looking and watching, then he thought of something else and looked away.

They had walked another 50' looking for the name *Harold* on a headstone. They saw *Henry, Horatio, Howard* but no *Harold*.

Somewhere as if far away, across a large field of wheat, he heard Ms. Yuka saying:

"Allan Pinkerton started the Pinkerton detective agency in 1850 in the Midwest.

"He was born in Glasgow, Scotland, and was the son of a Glasgow policeman. Yes Brenda, you can go to the bathroom."

Harold never answered Elizabeth's question about why he was quite often talking about being dead.

He didn't answer because he knew it was from spending so much time with his grandfather and just because he liked Elizabeth that didn't mean he had to answer all her questions.

He learned that from his grandfather too.

"Harold, I'm happy to be here looking for a headstone with your name on it."

"Thank you, Elizabeth. By the way did I ever tell you that I consider myself plural?"

"No you didn't."

"To me thinking and the fact that I'm my own best friend is plural.

"When you 'think' you are having a conversation with yourself. There are two—you and your thoughts.

"Which I see separately therefore plural. Within within. It's kind of like 'The Tennessee Waltz.'"

"Oh, I see."

Said Elizabeth as he imagined her thinking of throwing hatchets at him while he was sleeping.

Beautiful New England snowflakes started falling down like a trillion tiny analogies.

"Elizabeth, there's about 8" of snow.

"If it was rain it would be about 2".

"If it was dollhouse furniture it would be enough to fill 15,000 miniature apartments in Amsterdam."

Harold remembered going to the museum of science.

"Elizabeth, wouldn't it be interesting if there was a little button on the side of the headstones and if you pushed it you could hear a little moment of that person's life?

"Like this one here, this little girl Tanya only lived to be 8 years old in the mid-1800s.

"If there was a button to push you might hear:

"'I don't think it's cold I love it!'

"'Tanya come out now it's starting to rain.'

"'So what I'm already wet now! I'm swimming!

"'Look how it looks when the drops hit the water!!!'"

"What would you want to be heard so far in your life if there was a button on the side of your headstone, Harold?"

"I'd like to hear that first cry when I was born and they slapped me.

"What would you want to hear when they pushed your button?"

"I would like to hear the time I tickled my baby brother to the point he peed his diaper.

"My mother was mad at first then she started laughing too."

They continued walking in Harold's mind in the cemetery looking at the beautiful trees covered in snow along the way.

A stork that was addicted to birth control pills and cocaine and whiskey with no signs of being hammered flew directly through the rectangle causing Harold to wonder:

How many weddings the people in here had?

And whenever the two people said "I do" that meant both their names would be on the same headstone.

He was sure that didn't enter their mind on that very special day.

As they walked Harold's foot hit something. He knelt down and brushed the snow away.

It was a rusty old steel doorknob.

They both swept the light powdery snow away with their mittens.

The door was a little smaller than a regular size door. It was made of dark petrified wood surrounded in a black steel frame.

Harold tried to turn the knob but it only moved a little bit.

He kept trying harder and harder until it turned, but when he went to pull the door up it wouldn't move at all.

He tried three more times and up it came.

When the door opened a light came on like a refrigerator but it wasn't white it seemed to be colors.

Years later as an adult when someone would say to Harold:

"Hey could you help me move this couch?"

He would say:

"No, my back."

"Oh you have a sore back?"

"No I don't have a sore back."

There were wooden stairs going down on a steep angle about 10' down.

"Should we go down, Harold?"

"Well it's not that I want to go down it's that I don't not want to go down."

"You freak let's just go. Can't you just answer a question like a normal person for once!"

She said it in a kidding way as if she was mad but it was borderline.

Harold started going down the stairs.

He smiled when he noticed the nice pine railing had little

paintings of all kinds of birds on it, they were about 3" or 4" long.

The snowflakes were coming down with them.

When they reached the bottom the floor was 10" wide mahogany planks.

They were in a room 15' by 12' with a 6' high ceiling.

The first thing they noticed were the Christmas tree lights running along the very top of the wall.

The lights were all different colors, the small bulbs that everybody knows.

By the way the guy who invented that when you open a refrigerator door the light inside comes on hung himself in a Holiday Inn in Tampa, Florida, April 1961.

In the room there were two rocking chairs made of dark wood facing each other, about 5' apart.

Both of them were very beautiful, they were not identical. Elizabeth and Harold just stood there looking around at the place.

What got their attention most was the sound of the ocean. It sounded strong like on a little bit of a windy day.

The sound was on the other side of all four walls.

The cemetery was nowhere near any sea.

A South African Anndel Themil bird found only around the Indian Ocean which went extinct 10,000 years ago, and incidentally went extinct on purpose because it just could not take the bullshit anymore, flew through the rectangle causing Harold to think that the sound of moving water was actually the sound of time.

"Elizabeth, why don't we take a seat in these nice chairs and have a little chat."

The 7 year old people sat down.

On the wall opposite them were two small paintings, framed in very nice light brown wood.

One was of a small girl in a rowboat. You couldn't tell if the boat was on water or just floating in the air. She looked waifish, like someone from a Charles Dickens book.

Her hands were on the oars as if she was rowing or maybe resting, but you couldn't tell which it was for sure because like all paintings it wasn't moving.

Which reminded Harold that even movies aren't really moving. So in a way all movies were false advertising.

The other painting was of a lighthouse at the edge of a cliff overlooking very rough seas and it appeared to be on fire.

The fire was mostly at the top and down part of the side opposite the water.

The paintings seemed to have nothing to do with each other except for the water, which is probably how different species of fish feel.

"Elizabeth, which painting do you like better?"

"I'm not sure but look at that toy train on the floor over there."

There was a toy train resting on about 10' of straight track. Most trains circle around, this one didn't.

Harold thought of his own Lionel train set and how a few months ago he had the idea of gluing a couple of live ants to the tracks and running them over with his 6-car freight train.

He did not share this with Elizabeth, a decision he learned from his grandfather about "keeping things to yourself."

He smiled remembering when he thought of train garages. The idea of train garages made him laugh.

He didn't tell Elizabeth that either.

Harold figured that one of the most important parts of the brain had to be the part that helps you decide what to say and what not to say.

He figured that lots of times there was almost no control over your thinking but what to communicate was very much controllable.

It could keep you from being beat up or going to jail or being elected to public office.

Then they heard very quietly in the distance children playing at the beach.

Screams and laughing mixed in with the sound of waves and the sound of seagulls and the very faraway sound of a single engine plane.

"Do you hear that?"

"Yes Elizabeth, I do."

"This is a pretty weird situation don't you think?"

"Basically yes."

"Do you think I'm a mind reader, Harold?"

"No, I know you're not."

"Why not?"

"Because if you were you wouldn't be here."

That last interaction was completely for his own amusement.

Elizabeth had a tiny tiny smile like a beginner smile, like a baby having one of its first smiles. Imagine a little baby smiling for the very first time.

It's happened to every baby, every baby all over the world. Babies are very weird creatures.

Harold remembered the first time he ever yawned, he thought he had lost control of his mouth.

He loved the sounds of summer at the beach coming from the other side of every wall.

As if that was the season underground in the cemetery. That could make the idea of dying not as negative.

Maybe even appealing. Maybe.

He loved summer so much and thought it was magical.

Moosehead Lake with his grandfather was like being in a dream.

He thought God, if there was a God, put extra effort into creating that time of year.

Many many years later he would love the summers on a beautiful little island in the North Atlantic.

On the wall to the right about 5' up were two stethoscopes hanging on hooks.

He got up out of his chair and went over to look at them.

He took one off and stuck the ends in his ears and put the other end over his heart and listened and then slowly started dancing a waltz to his own heartbeat.

Elizabeth got up out of her chair, walked over and put the other stethoscope in her ears and the end over her heart. Harold stopped dancing.

They were just standing there, both of them looking down at the floor and concentrating on the machine that grew on its own inside them.

At the same time they looked up at each other and without saying anything put the end of each other's stethoscope over the other one's heart and listened.

Harold wasn't sure but he thought Elizabeth's heart was beating a little bit faster than his and Elizabeth wasn't sure but she thought Harold's heart was beating a little bit slower than hers.

He thought if their hearts were clocks one of them would be considered wrong.

Then he realized that their hearts were both correct therefore there must be different speeds and measurements of time that were also correct.

They smiled at each other.

Then Harold thought that death was a giant "time-out" but he kept it to himself because he didn't want to break the moment.

Chapter 6

A stunning Albino Blackbird glided through the rectangle with an emotionless face like the look that some very beautiful women have because they're so used to men of all ages looking at them with their mouths open in awe and even though they love that the men are looking at them they act like it doesn't matter to them and some of them even act like the men are actually rude for looking at them and some of these women will experience an emotional self-esteem plane crash when time washes their beauty away like someone cleaning the sand off a sidewalk with a garden hose.

This bird suggested that he and Elizabeth drink more coffee so it would affect their hearts and it would stimulate the dancing to each other's beats.

They did and started tapping their toes to their internal sounds, looking at each other smiling even more.

The coffee sped up their hearts like their souls could hear banjo music.

By now Ms. Yuka was a distant memory although she was only 25' away and he was looking right at her.

There she was with her beautiful very plain looking face.

The way she was way older than everyone in the class fascinated him. And it was because of time.

Once in a movie Harold saw a guy reading the London *Times* and the headline read:

"Time Will No Longer Tell"

A bird made of clear water about the size of a falcon flew through the rectangle without spilling a drop causing Harold to say:

"Elizabeth, exactly when did you stop being a baby?"

The boy was playing with her mind for his own amusement.

No response.

She heard him even though she had the stethoscope in her ears because everything doesn't have to make sense.

Just look at the world and your life.

"Harold, do you want put our stethoscopes up to the wall and listen?"

Harold looked into her blue eyes because they were the only eyes she had and said:

"No Elizabeth, I think that would be an invasion of privacy.

"In fact I think all of archeology is an invasion of privacy.

"People should have respect for the dead."

"Oh I kind of see what you mean. Well could you tell me the dream about when you were accidentally adopted by your own parents?"

Then the blonde haired girl imitated a black haired girl

smiling and the water bird inside Harold's head drank himself and disappeared and laughed while he was doing it.

"Ok so in the dream my parents are very young and not married yet when they have me and they don't think they're ready to raise a child so they give me up for adoption.

"Then about two years after getting married they feel they're ready for a child and they decide to adopt one because since they already made one themselves they think this will balance it out and so they go to a different adoption agency and there had been a lot of paperwork mix-ups and confusion and their actual child, meaning me, had been sent over there with a different name and all different information and they adopt him and bring him home and then about 3 years later the adoption agencies realize the mistake and they tell my parents.

"And one day my parents bring me into the living room and say:

"'Harold, we have something very important to tell you— you are not really adopted.'

"I look at them blankly like a professional mannequin.

"'Well actually what we mean is, you are adopted but by us who are your real parents.'

"'Do you mean to tell me that I was adopted by my biological parents?'

"And they say:

"'Yes.'

"Then I turn my head and look out the picture window and out on the street I see a small herd of yellow papier-mâché ponies running by in slow motion then I wake up."

"That's really extremely strange, Harold. And what do you think that means?"

"I think it means sometimes you can't even trust yourself."

And they both would have lived happily ever after if they had died right then and there. But they didn't.

Harold then motioned with his left hand, even though he was right-handed, to Elizabeth suggesting to sit back down in the rocking chair and she did and then he did and then they both took the stethoscopes out of their ears.

They looked like two 7 year old surgeons taking a break in the doctors' lounge.

Harold thought of saying:

"Elizabeth, if you were a well respected surgeon and there were twins just born in the hospital and the parents were insane and they wanted to pay you a huge amount of money to sew the children together to make Siamese twins about how much would they have to pay you to do that?" But he didn't.

Instead he said:

"Elizabeth, if you could ask the people on the other side of this room a question about their life and how they would live differently if they could live again what would it be?"

"I would ask them that."

She continued:

"Harold, you didn't answer me before when I asked you why you think about being dead so much?"

"Because somehow, and I'm not sure how, I think there's something to learn about being alive if you think about it being over and then work backwards."

Softly they heard the ocean and children playing and screaming and seagulls and a single engine plane and they could hear that the sky was blue.

Harold learned from his grandfather that time was gold, that time was the most important thing about being alive, meaning what you did with your time.

His grandfather told him that rather than measuring time with clocks whenever you see a bird it can be a click, a nudge to be aware of your time, that a bird is like a live second hand.

Birds and the sound of water represent time.

With the combination of birds on the inside of his head and the ocean on the outside of his head Harold had lots of time reminders.

He wondered if birds had a little little rectangle inside their heads that had very tiny tiny birds flying through that caused their thoughts.

From the other side of the walls the sound of the ocean and children playing at the beach got a little louder.

Kids laughing and little fun sounding screams.

That very distinct summer happy beach sound mixed perfectly as if it was done by George Martin.

A sound known worldwide. International summer children playing beach sounds.

Harold thought that if he was ever being walked to the

electric chair he would ask for a recording of that sound to be played.

All the way to them strapping him in:

"Do you have any last words?"

Very relaxed casual stare and then:

"Sounds like a beautiful day. Take care bye-bye."

Then from behind the wall with the paintings, a little bit more than faintly in the underground distance, a child's voice:

"Elizabeth, come on over. It's so nice. Come on over!"

"Harold, did you hear that?"

"Yes. I'm sure it's just a coincidence that they said your name on the other side of that wall.

"I wouldn't worry about it and read some extra meaning into it like it's a weird premonition or something."

He said it while smiling which meant he didn't really mean what he just said. But not a lie.

Funny how that is.

Elizabeth looked at him in a concerned way like when you're on an airplane and you hear an unfamiliar noise.

Then after the crashing of another wave the voice of a different child:

"Wow Harold you're so close. We're all waiting, come on over it'll be really fun! Don't think about it, don't hesitate, just do it.

"You only live once. Hahaha!"

Harold sat stunned, frozen, he wondered if it was possible to cry internally so Elizabeth wouldn't see.

He wondered if it was possible to cry to death.

They sat facing each other with horrified looks on his and her faces.

Now the shoe was on the other foot. Now it was a different story. Now the ball was in his court.

Now the baby drank tequila.

Now the Mississippi River wrote letters to heaven.

Now the number 9 was removed.

Now the very beautiful Ingrid Bergman sat naked on Santa's lap.

Now all of China was radioactive and on sale.

Now all words were spelled the same.

He wanted to go back to the classroom, he felt like he was 20' underwater and he desperately needed to swim to the surface and take a big gulp of air.

He couldn't think of anything to say.

Just in the nick time a very rare Black Capped Chickadee that somehow resembled Walt Disney glided through the rectangle causing Harold to say:

"Elizabeth, being born is the beginning of borrowed time."

He looked at the toy train in a real trance and Elizabeth stared at him and the sound of the ocean and children and seagulls faded away and then slowly they heard the sound of tall trees being moved by a breeze and you could hear how they looked—50' tall New England type pine trees like the ones

Harold was always walking around in near his house, and then you could hear the sound of water lapping like water at a small lake, and you could hear the footsteps of a child walking on the leaves so it must be fall over there.

Ms. Yuka was now standing right next to Harold looking down at him.

"Harold, where are you? It's your turn to talk in front of the class."

He looked up at her and she could see his eyes were about a quarter of the way filled with tears.

"What? Talk about what?"

"Talk about something ironic."

From his point of view he could see her face over her perfect size breasts and it looked like it was just a head on a pair of tits and Harold thought, "What a wonderful world this is—I thank God for this moment, if there is a God."

He got up and walked toward the front of the class.

After several steps he passed Elizabeth sitting at her desk in her light blue sweater and turquoise barrette on the left side of her blonde head.

It seemed almost weird to see her actually sitting at her desk in the class instead of in a rocking chair with a stethoscope around her neck in an underground room in the cemetery.

She noticed him about as much as an ant notices a 747 flying overhead at 37,000'.

Which would be a pattern he would experience with girls and women many many times his whole life.

He got up to Ms. Yuka's desk and turned to face everybody and he could see that she had walked to the back of the class and was watching from there.

Harold decided not to be nervous because it would be easier that way.

He thought of what was just happening in the room in the cemetery with the sound of the breeze in the trees and water lapping and it reminded him of Walden Pond which was a few towns over from where he lived.

He looked at Elizabeth and she was looking at him.

Harold began to speak:

"I think it's ironic that every year thousands and thousands of people go to see where Henry Thoreau lived, a hermit. A famous hermit.

"I also find it very interesting that his father had a business making pencils and then Henry became a writer. God bless you—if there is a God."

Harold walked back to his seat and as he passed Elizabeth he very discreetly took in a deep breath to see if she had any kind of smell.

He inhaled so deeply that he got dizzy and almost bumped into Brenda's desk then he got back on track and continued to his seat as Ms. Yuka said:

"Very good, Harold."

Under his breath, very quietly for his own amusement he said:

"911, what's your emergency?"

He only smelled crayons and Elmer's glue but didn't think it was from Elizabeth.

Chapter 7

A rare dwarf nocturnal Vulture only found in the Serengeti who was the only bird known to man to have gone extinct and be abundant at the same time flew majestically through the rectangle in Harold's head with a stern confidence—not caring at all how society looked at him—like Bob Dylan when he went electric—and it caused Harold in his mind to say:

"I think that birth is child abuse."

Ms. Yuka was now walking back toward the front of the class and was about to say who the next peasant in her dictatorship would be who had to go up and dance like a stringless marionette until her mind was satisfied and Harold was hoping it would be the wingless angel Elizabeth.

From his conversations with his grandfather and comments he made he learned that being in love with someone was a very tricky thing and was like gambling with the idea of yourself.

It was a package deal of positive and negative emotions—a pendulum festival—like being served a birthday cake that might have poison in it.

Harold did not know what he meant and wouldn't know for many years. But then he would know.

You bet he would know.

Ms. Yuka stood off to the side of her desk and said:

"Ok Elizabeth, it's your turn."

Harold watched her get up as an Austrian yellow Cancrow flew through the rectangle like a very small F-16 made of meat and bone and beautiful silky feathers.

This bird was very insane causing Harold to imagine someone with red patent leather teeth.

Since Ms. Yuka was the only one facing him he saw the beautiful average looking teacher with a mouth full of gorgeous red patent leather teeth and he thought she looked fantastic.

As if Salvador Dalí was her dentist.

Sometimes Harold saw his mind as an insane asylum where none of the rooms had doors.

Incidentally Harold could not spell at all and once spelled the word *spell* with one *l*.

One time he was trying to write the word *weather* and he looked it up to make sure of how to spell it and he saw that he spelled it wrong by writing *wether*.

But he learned that was an actual word too which meant "a male sheep castrated before sexual maturity."

So after that sometimes when he heard people complaining about the weather under his breath he would say:

"It could be worse."

Elizabeth stood there as rays of sunlight came 93 million miles through the classroom windows and fell asleep on her blonde hair and blonde skin and blue eyes and white teeth and Harold couldn't believe that something that far away was in on the plan to make him like her even more.

She began to speak:

"I think that it's ironic that every new invention that makes our life better also makes it worse.

"Like the invention of cars is a good thing but before that there was no traffic and no car accidents.

"The invention of phones is a good thing but before that you were never yelled at for being on the phone too long.

"And being born is a good thing but now you have to worry about dying. Thank you."

She sat down at her desk as Ms. Yuka said:

"Very good Elizabeth, that was very interesting."

Harold as usual very quietly to himself under his breath said:

"How dare you judge her."

Ms. Yuka was talking but Harold wasn't listening because he was picturing her turned into a canary with a piece of string tied to her skinny bird ankle and him holding the other end like in the famous Goya painting—

Boy With Bird.

If this was a painting it would be called—

Boy With Teacher Turned Into Bird.

He imagined that even though she was now a bird she was still aware that she was Ms. Yuka and could still talk.

Bird Ms. Yuka would be yelling:

"Harold, get me off this string and find someone to turn me back into a person!"

"Shut up or I'll piss on you. By the way you would look good as a Koel."

A Koel is a bird native to the Asian part of the world. Harold can't remember where he learned this.

"If this was WWII I'd give you some bird nylons and some chocolates. The kind of nylons with the seam going down the back.

"We could be in a hotel room in Paris all smashed on red wine and I would be getting a kick out of you all drunk trying to straighten your nylons out with the tips of your wings."

The sound of the waves crashed again and the sound of the children and seagulls returned and Harold was back in the room again with Elizabeth.

Sitting in the rocking chairs they looked down and saw

the 14 tiny yellow horses grazing on the floor on a field of tiny grass.

Off to one end of the field of tiny grass there was a very small old worn out brown stagecoach with old faded red curtains in the windows.

It had the two wooden rails that would have gone on the side of the horses, coming out the front and went on an angle down to the ground.

Scattered all around it were five tiny tumbleweeds.

Harold prayed that he was either insane or not insane.

That way he knew his prayers would be answered.

He didn't pray to God, if there was a God, because he didn't want to be a hypocrite.

The End.

Not really.

An extremely blue bluebird flew through the rectangle and Harold remembered that in January Ms. Yuka was taking the class on a field trip to the planetarium.

Harold loved the planetarium but thought it would be better if there were birds in the sky and maybe clouds and wind.

He remembered how his grandfather told him that the Lakota thought a planetarium was ridiculous and that only the white man would build an indoor sky and charge money to look at it.

Harold thought that maybe he could sit beside Elizabeth when they went.

Maybe he could lean over to her during the lecture or presentation or whatever it's called and quietly whisper:

"Look I'm building a spaceship and all I need is one more triple-A battery and that should do it.

"So the main reason I came on this field trip, other than I had to, was to get a good look at the stars to help me figure out where I might be headed, and you can come with me if you want to baby I think it'll be fun.

"I figured if you told your parents you'd be gone for a few hours we could go away for 35 years and be back in 10 seconds.

"One thing I'd like to do is get a look at the Big Dipper from the other side and other than that kind of play it by ear.

"Have you ever held hands on a spaceship before sweetie?

"I mean I know you're only 7 and I'm not saying you've been around but I think we'd have a good time."

The first time Harold went to a planetarium was in first grade which was two years ago, a long time ago. The place had just opened.

Harold can still remember the smell the seats had because they were new. A kind of a sweet chemical green plastic type smell that he liked.

After being in the planetarium whenever he looked up at the stars he could smell the seats and it seemed like the stars had a smell to them.

Actually in everything he ever heard about astronomy

he never heard anything about the smell of planets or the universe.

He thought it would have to be a nice smell and that it could be used as a compliment.

"Sweetie you smell like the universe, you really do."

The first time he was there at the end of the lecture the guy asked if anyone had any questions. Harold raised his hand.

"Yes?"

"What do you think God would think of the quality of this planetarium?"

"Well I really don't know the answer to that."

Harold under his breath:

"I'm shocked."

A black African Scottish rainbow beaked Teranipitin flew through the rectangle and kept doing small circles behind Harold's eyes causing him to focus on the overwhelming situation of man knowing almost nothing.

He then realized that the daytime sky was created for one purpose only and that was so you could not see the universe for several hours.

To Harold it was like giving candy to a screaming baby to distract it from a traumatic situation.

The pretty blue sky and the puffy white clouds.

No stars. No universe. No infinity.

That's why children were afraid of the dark, they were instinctively horrified by absolutely no answers.

Especially no answers if you took the concept of God out of the picture.

At his first trip to the planetarium the class went into the gift shop after the lecture and Harold bought a map of the universe that was about the size of a road map.

Even at 7 he knew it was impossible to have a map of the universe and thought it was actually rude to be selling such a thing.

He thought this as he purchased it.

While Harold's class was in the gift shop David Ingram was caught trying to steal a foam rubber Mars and got into a lot of trouble.

Harold thought that's too bad, his grandfather should have paid for it in advance.

Random Harold thoughts:

"There's never two yesterdays in a row."

"The problem with fat people is they never eat on an empty stomach."

"A Timex suicide watch."

Chapter 8

The synthetic experience and conversation Harold had with Elizabeth at the cemetery reminded him of a reoccurring dream that he only had once.

He knew and prayed that he would have it again and again.

The boy saw it as an investment, like when people buy a piece of land that will be worth way more later.

In the dream Harold is sitting at an outdoor cafe on the moon.

There's no actual building it's just about 20 black tables with 2 or 3 black chairs at each one sitting on the grey surface.

Harold is seated at one of the tables that's off to the side of course. With his back to the universe.

He never knew if he was facing north or south or east or west because he wasn't sure if those directions applied if you were no longer on the earth.

And how the hell would he know anyway?—he was only 7.

His chair faced the other tables and chairs and if he looked to his left he saw the blue and white earth way in the distance, like that picture taken from *Apollo 17*.

The picture known as *The Blue Marble*.

Harold was wearing a faded red corduroy shirt, which was the same color as a Lakota's memory, and black pants.

Moving quickly around the empty tables as if the place was extremely busy and wearing a long sleeve white shirt and black pants was the waitress.

5'8" tall, medium build and sweaty even though there was no atmosphere.

The fast way she moved looked to Harold how fish would move in a tank full of adrenaline rather than water.

She was walking around wiping off tables even though there was nothing on them and pushing the chairs in evenly even though they didn't seem to be off in the first place.

Harold looked past her into the galaxy of total darkness and stars thinking he was happy to be away from the earth for a while, away from the stress of his 7 year old life and Ms. Yuka and her class.

He looked again at the blue marble, thought of Ms. Yuka and gave the finger toward the earth. But not to the earth, to the teacher.

Then he quietly laughed to himself because he actually liked Ms. Yuka and it really wasn't her fault that she's the teacher and had to order people around.

He looked out up to the galaxy for a few seconds and then lowered his gaze to the ponytailed head of the waitress that was continuing to do what she was doing and getting closer to his table.

He noticed there was no music playing at this cafe and he

wondered if it was because music can't play without atmosphere or if there was just no music playing.

He thought, "What a world this is," then he thought that's another term that might not apply if you're not on the earth.

He also remembered he thought that birth was child abuse and smiled to himself.

He imagined writing a poem called "Birth is Child Abuse" by Harold.

And if The Big Bang was the birth of the universe then "The Big Bang was Universe Abuse"—another poem by Harold, grade 3.

Incidentally The Big Bang theory pissed Harold off and he thought it was childish and longed for one day to address these naïve scientists.

Now the waitress came over and stood at Harold's table.

"How are you little boy?

"What a nice day to be on the moon. Can I get you something?

"All we have is water and it's a little bit different than the water you're used to because it's H_3O.

"So it has kind of a sweet taste to it, I think you'll like it. Would you like to try it?"

"Yes please."

Harold watched her pour water into a blue glass from a blue pitcher that she didn't have when she walked over and then she said:

"There you go, let me know how you like it."

He took a sip as he looked up at her and thought how beautiful she was with part of the Milky Way behind her and then said:

"I like it, thank you. Why is it sweeter than regular water?"

"It's sweeter because the third H is for honey."

She was smiling at him.

An absolutely stunning beautiful Polish girl/woman with big grey/green eyes that seemed like they could have easily fit perfectly on the face of a large African cat then she calmly said:

"You know I may or may not be a mind reader."

Harold felt the blood rushing and wondered if he was really turning red.

He wondered how certain pieces of blood knew where and when to go in his body and he had to try to find that out.

He was mesmerized by this girl/woman. She smiled very natural and real.

He had to say something.

"How long have you been a waitress on the moon?"

She had a quiet casual self-assured but not arrogant way about her.

"I started when I was in college and then when I graduated I stayed on so I've been working here for about three years. I'm thinking I may want to travel before I get a real job.

"You know go to Europe, maybe Amsterdam and Paris."

"Oh."

In his mind he thought, "She's already on the moon and she wants to travel."

He thought of Neil Armstrong arguing with his wife after the Apollo:

"Don't you understand I DO NOT WANT TO GO ANY-WHERE!"

"Do you mind if I sit down for a minute? My feet are killing me even though there's no gravity."

"Ok."

She did and Harold noticed that her hands were dirty from holding money but there was no money or anyone else in sight.

She extended her slightly filthy hand that had the look of a London wench pub worker from the 1800s and said:

"My name is Tinga what's your name?"

He put his suburban 1960s boy hand into hers to shake it and because of how he was very aware of everything times a billion her skin had the feel of a perfumed electric fence.

"Harold."

"Oh that's a nice name, why did they name you Harold?"

"I'm named after my uncle Toby."

She did not blink.

"When he was a little boy he would have nightmares and he kept saying the name Harold over and over in his sleep."

She just kept looking at him smiling and started to ruin his life.

"That's a funny story."

This person was so pretty that she made him nervous and he just didn't understand why.

Little did he know this was just the beginning of all that bullshit.

Her eyes were magnificent compared to his but he was still very appreciative that his worked perfectly.

Two piss holes in the snow.

In Harold's head the factory part of the brain that was in charge of speech manufactured the following sentence:

"Is the moon closer to the sun than the earth is?"

He knew it was the same. He was testing her.

Harold noticed the twinkle from the Milky Way on her simple silver earrings.

"They are the same average distance."

"Very nice," was his thought.

He kept looking all around taking everything in. Tinga poured herself a glass of water.

"Do you ever get lonely up here all by yourself?"

"Oh no I never get lonely no matter where I am because there's so much going on in my head and I think in everyone's head. To me the human brain is a portable universe."

"Yes I agree," said the 7 year old boy.

He continued:

"Well if the universe is expanding I wonder if our brains

are expanding? Is that a birdhouse way over there? See over there?"

He pointed with his left hand on the end of his arm that was a perfect size for his body.

"Oh yes it is."

"Is there ever a bird in it? I mean do you ever see a bird flying over there?"

Harold looked back toward the earth and before Tinga could answer it started snowing very gently.

The image Harold saw was the blue marble through the white snowflakes falling onto the surface of the grey moon.

"I've only seen one bird over there intermittently," Tinga said. "It looks like a yellow and black sparrow but I'm not sure."

Then Harold said, "You know that Big Bang theory pisses me off because that's supposed to be the start of everything, but what was before that?

"I think the scientists are like nursery school kids wearing suits and making shit up and having press conferences and everyone is taking notes."

He realized he would have to figure out how to have this dream again. A person's dreams are up to them.

An extremely rare bilingual Irish Kola Cresta sparrow whose life's span was 72 hours caused Harold to wonder if time was different on the moon then maybe he could marry the waitress.

He said, "It's so quiet here."

She smiled showing her shiny beautiful woman teeth.

If it was in a toothpaste commercial they would say:

"Makes your teeth whiter than the snow on the moon."

"Yes it is. It's nice and empty here because it's so hard to get to. Like Telluride, Colorado.

"I hope it never gets built-up here because it will ruin the charm."

Harold looked at her jet black hair, darker than Ms. Yuka's, darker than the photos of the Lakota that his grandfather once showed him.

He was trying to judge which was darker her hair or the blackness of the universe behind her.

Now he felt it would be sad and disrespectful to God, if there was a God, to only have this dream once.

An incredibly rare red and black spotted Appalachian Seagull glided gently through the rectangle causing the following idea:

As Harold looked back at the earth he thought of the globe in his classroom and wouldn't it be great if the earth had some fun and used the equator as a jump rope for about 5 or 10 minutes a month.

Then maybe everyone would be happy and all the wars would end. For a few minutes. Yeah, sure.

In regards to marrying her, he thought he should act fast because he might wake up.

He pictured this interaction with someone:

"I thought you were getting married?"

"I was but then I woke up."

Tinga looked into his eyes.

"Harold, do you know that time is different on the moon?"

His inner aura smiled like a young boy getting out of the car in the parking lot of Disneyland.

"No, I didn't know but I was wondering about it."

He thought maybe she was just making conversation.

He remembered his grandfather telling him he once knew a guy who was accidentally killed trying to make conversation out of wood.

Harold never lied but didn't mention the part about wanting to marry her.

It was drilled into him by his mother not to ever lie or steal anything ever.

He was very obedient to what she said. It was ingrained into his character forever.

Years later when he was no longer a boy, he realized his mother was a consistent liar and thief. A total hypocrite. But he stayed completely honest.

She once said to him, "Honesty is the best policy." Then she told him she made that up.

Her hypocrisy was just a tiny tiny version of Religion and Government.

And the politician fucking soulless asshole low-life scumbags that are at the top of the negative side of the list on whether or not there is a God.

111

When Harold became aware of how politicians on TV refused to answer a question directly, it infuriated him and he thought someone should come out of the wings and ask them this:

"Do you agree that you are not answering the question?"

Then no matter what he says he should be beaten until he's unconscious on live television with no criminal consequences.

That should bring an end to this behavior that's disrespectful of the mind of anyone older than a fucking toddler.

Image:

Sixteen pirate ships out at sea at night completely engulfed in flames full of live politicians.

Slowly the snow slowed down until it stopped.

A rare Spanish rabbit bird, only found in Singapore in the early part of the 17th century, flew through the rectangle bringing a couple of thoughts:

How different snow would be if the flakes made loud banging noises when they hit the ground.

Like smashing coffee cups.

How different it would be if, when boats pulled huge nets out of the ocean full of thousands of fish, the fish were screaming in horror.

God made some pretty interesting adjustments to lots of situations.

If there was a God.

But not enough. Not enough. Not enough.

He thought:

"Who am I to judge God? God made me, that's who. If there is a God."

A chameleon bird flew through the rectangle that can't really be described because it keeps changing.

"Tinga, how do you feel about the universe?"

"I think it's underrated."

She laughed and Harold smiled.

"How do you feel about it, Harold?"

"I don't think man will ever figure out how it works because of the level of the human mind."

"What do you mean?"

"It would be like putting a baby into the cockpit of an F-16 and expecting him to land on an aircraft carrier at night in the rain.

"And I don't think the brain will physiologically evolve enough to understand before man goes extinct or ever. That's how I feel."

Tinga looked at him with her stunning eyes and Harold wondered if like a new car a new brain had a new brain smell.

He imagined that Tinga was so impressed with what he'd just said that she would want to smell his young brain.

"That's very interesting Harold, especially coming from a boy with such a young brain.

"By the way, have you noticed anything about the sense of smell on the moon?"

"No, I hadn't noticed."

"Well, when I first got here I couldn't smell anything, but after a while you do smell lots of things.

"The craters smell like birch trees and sometimes there's the smell of burning wood, like from a fireplace."

Harold was shocked by this—or maybe Tinga was insane.

She and her stunning eyes looked at him and he was fascinated he didn't melt.

Then she slowly leaned forward so her nose was just above his forehead, exactly at his light brown hairline.

She said:

"Excuse me, do you mind if I sniff your brain?"

Harold was looking right at her neck and he knew that skin was connected to the entire rest of her body.

His being was silently blasting the sound of a WWII air raid siren.

She was so beautiful insanity would not be a drawback. In fact it might add to the situation.

She appeared to have a nuclear-powered twinkle in her eye.

"What?"

He really heard her, he just wanted to hear her say it again.

"Do you mind if I sniff your brain?"

His mind began to race but went nowhere because there was no better place to be.

"No, I don't mind."

He heard her sniffing the top of his head like a rabbit.

Several quick sniffs: *sniff sniff sniff sniff sniff sniff sniff*.

Harold could feel his blood now moving and he was hoping it only made him blush.

She smelled too. Like a 22 year old girl. He tried to place that smell but he couldn't.

It seemed like a mixture of skin lotion and confidence.

She leaned back, looked into his eyes, and said:

"Hmm, very very nice, Harold. Like the interior of a new '65 Mustang, standard four-on-the-floor. Right out of the factory."

She looked toward the earth.

"Thank you for letting me do that."

"You're welcome."

He voted in his head that her profile was equally as beautiful as seeing her straight-on.

"Harold, did you know that in Russia there are 11 different time zones?"

"No, I did not know that."

"I'm surprised, I would think you would know that with a brain that smells like yours. I've never been there but I want to go."

"Well, I hope someday you get to go."

"Thank you Harold, you're such a nice boy."

When she wasn't looking, he winked at her.

Harold started fidgeting in his chair and nervously looking around at the galaxy.

"What's the matter, Harold? I think I know but you tell me."

She smiled at him which she was so good at.

"I know at some point I'm going to wake up and I don't want to."

"Well Harold, are you aware of the Lakota Indians?"

"Yes."

He knew she knew he was.

"There's a ritual they have in order to return to a dream and have it continue. Maybe you could find out what it is."

"Do you know what it is?"

"No, if I knew I would tell you."

She just looked at him long enough to make him feel more uncomfortable, then very very quietly so no one else in the galaxy could hear she said:

"I'll tell you one thing, if this was my dream I wouldn't want to wake up either."

Harold remembered standing outside with his grandfather at Moosehead Lake in Maine during a lunar eclipse at about 2:00 in the morning the night his grandfather turned 73.

They had a fire going and were looking up at the sky. Tall and thin wearing old clothes, a greenish black coat that went to his thighs, his grandfather had a full head of long greyish white hair and about 3 weeks of grey white whiskers.

"Harold, see what's happening up there? Those same elements you see are also in the fire right here, and in you and me.

"We're made of the same things they're just in a different order.

"Like a jigsaw puzzle that can be made more than one way. You can have your own eclipse in your mind.

"In fact you will have many in your lifetime. When something blocks out your whole world for a little while and then it just goes."

In the distance a train whistle. "In your mind is the present and dreams and daydreams and the past.

"Like in the world of the Lakota that still exists, even though it isn't here, you can go from one to the other whenever you want, like taking a walk in the sky.

"It's all very magical, Harold. Really an amazing thing that all these elements came together and made you and are you.

"As the scientist Carl Sagan wrote:

"'Complex microscopic architectures in which the carbon atom plays a central role.'"

Harold looked up at him and to the right of his head he saw the eclipse.

"Here's something else, Harold,

"'The Present is a Past factory.'"

Briefly Harold's grandfather envied the fact that Harold had no idea of what he was talking about.

He thought the amount that the boy did not know was beautiful and an entire different way of being alive.

He wondered if it was possible to be in your 70s and have the perspective of a 5 year old without being nuts.

When Harold was in his 70s he would know it was possible.

Harold watched Tinga as she looked out at the Milky Way.

"Tinga."

"Yes, Harold."

"Have you ever been here during a lunar eclipse?"

"That's funny."

"My grandfather would love it here."

"That birdhouse over there reminds me of him. He built a few that had fire escapes on them.

"He taught me about cameras and we would take black and white pictures of the birdhouses and other things.

"He had many boxes of color photographs taken by Ansel Adams.

"Ansel had given them to him. He told my grandfather he was color-blind that's why he preferred black and white pictures.

"One night after drinking some whiskey he told me a story about a man he knew in Europe who was cleaning out his many hundred year old barn and way up on the third level he found several trunks that contained all the lyrics to all the classical music.

"Hundreds and hundreds of pages of lyrics.

"A Rimsky-Korsakov lyric was the only one he could remember:

"'Baby you have the wrong eyes.'"

"He seems like a very interesting person, Harold."

"Interesting people find him interesting."

"Thank you."

"Tinga, you know that old saying about the moon being made out of cheese?"

"Yes."

"Do you know how that got started?"

"No Harold, I don't. Why, do you?"

"No."

Tinga had no reaction to this because she was briefly thinking about something else which was how old she was when she changed from taking baths to showers.

Incidentally Harold read somewhere that Ernest Hemingway had a swimming pool at his house in Key West and that Ava

Gardner once swam in it and after she was gone he instructed the pool maintenance people to not ever change the water.

An adolescent African Janca flew through the rectangle:

"Tinga, imagine how different the universe would look without the stars? Imagine looking up at night and you see nothing but total darkness."

"Oh you mean like on a cloudy night?"

"Haha."

Chapter 9

"Harold, what grade are you in?"

It was an abstract question but he knew what she meant.

"Third."

It reminded him of when people are on the witness stand on TV and the guy says:

"Do you swear to tell the whole truth and nothing but the truth so help you God?"

This is what Harold would say in this situation:

"First of all if there is a God.

"Secondly the idea of the whole truth and nothing but the truth is just so innocent and naïve it's like asking me to describe the entire universe without going into detail."

"Do you like your teacher?"

"Yes."

"What do you like about her?"

"She's generally pretty fair and I like her teeth. She has red patent leather teeth."

No response then:

"Harold, do you want to go for a walk? I know this place that would be good for a lake. It's over that hill over there."

She pointed past Harold, past the birdhouse on the pole to about 20 craters away.

Harold thought it was good that birds never have to buy a birdhouse.

"It's nice. We would be facing the opposite direction of the earth."

For some reason Harold wished that a bird would fly through the rectangle. He didn't know if he should go or not.

Something told him it was time to wake up. His grand-father told him he would wake up many times in his life, maybe this was one of them.

He thought of asking her if anyone ever told her she looked like Loretta Lynn.

But he didn't because he knew no one ever did because she didn't look anything like Loretta Lynn.

This made Harold laugh to himself. It also made him again think that maybe he was insane.

"Ok Tinga, let's go."

They both got up and started walking.

She was to his right and so was the earth. Their shoes made the same crunching sound as when you walk on a few inches of snow.

Soon they were passing the birdhouse on the pole. Harold looked up at the hole that was in the front, no bird.

"I found the spot we're going to a few weeks ago. I just felt like going for a walk, you know, to stretch my legs."

He didn't know.

Just then something happened that never happened to Harold before.

Coming from behind them a bird flew right over and at the same exact time that same type of bird flew through the rectangle.

Cardinals. Harold thought, "What are the chances of that?"

It was almost like there was a three-dimensional shadow of the bird inside his head. He wondered if there could be three-dimensional shadows.

He wondered if there was a way to make a shadow darker.

And if so—why would anyone want that?

The thought the cardinal brought Harold was that maybe Tinga was going to leave him alone on the moon.

But he thought—does it really matter? He's in a dream. He felt that it still mattered. He didn't want to be left alone on the moon.

They continued to walk hearing their footsteps.

In the distance Harold swore he heard the ocean like he did when he was in the room at the cemetery with Elizabeth.

The beauty of a dream, life minus logic.

Even in life lots of times there is no logic. Lots and lots of times. Lots of times.

He thought if he ever met God, if there was a God, he would say to him:

"Where's the logic?"

"We're about halfway there, Harold. I know you hear the ocean, I hear it too."

Harold was a little bit behind her.

He was 7, if he was in his 20s he would be watching her ass, thinking, "What a great ass.

"God made that ass. If there is a God."

Then he would have thought:

"It's still a great ass even if there is no God."

"Tinga."

"Yes Harold."

"Can I ask you a personal question?"

"Yes."

"Do you know what time it is? No I'm just kidding. Do you think the moon is closer to God than the earth is? If there is a God."

She was catching on to this boy and his mind.

"Yes Harold. The moon is about 500' closer to God than the earth."

She grinned like a leopard having his balls tickled.

"Haha."

Harold smiled internally and externally so neither side of him would get jealous. That thought made him smile too. His head was a circus.

It was like the day he was born someone handed him a ticket to his brain.

They walked about a quarter of a mile and then came to a ridge of a wide-open circular area. It looked like a huge crater about 10,000' across.

And yes it did look like an empty lake.

"Here we are, Harold. I wish it was full of water."

Harold wondered if it was full of water would it be H_3O. He thought his grandfather would like this if it was a lake.

He could imagine him saying to someone:

"I'll be back in a month. I'm going to the lake on the moon."

The two of them stood on the rim of the crater.

There they were—the 7 year old boy and the Polish moon princess waitress.

The crater casually sloped down about 100' then leveled off flat.

Without saying anything Tinga stepped over the edge and started walking down the hill.

Harold stood frozen watching her like he was watching the emotion of sadness.

When she got to the bottom she started running straight across—her beautiful thick jet black hair past her shoulders flowing in the non atmosphere.

As he shockingly watched her running he looked all the way across the crater to the other side, at the very top he saw what appeared to be a horse with a rider.

It was so little in the distance, about an inch tall.

Harold squinted and he recognized the colors the person on the horse was wearing and knew it was Lakota. Mostly red and black.

As Tinga was getting smaller and smaller she suddenly stopped and turned around.

She was so little standing in the middle of this giant wide-open space. It looked like a shot in a David Lean movie.

Then she waved her hand high above her head and yelled:

"Goodbye, Harold, goodbye! Take care of yourself!"

She quickly turned around and continued running really fast. Not fast enough to have the Doppler effect but very fast.

He wondered if anyone could run fast enough to have the Doppler effect.

His grandfather told him that getting old was the human version of it.

Harold watched and felt tears coming into his eyes. He looked back at the earth.

There was a photograph of the earth called *The Pale Blue Dot* taken from the *Voyager 1* space probe from 3.7 billion miles away. Less than one pixel, an extremely tiny speck.

Being on the moon he was way closer to the earth than that. 238,900 miles.

So comparatively if Tinga rides away on the back of the Lakota's horse he still won't be lonely.

Note: If you're wondering how Harold would know of this photograph since it wasn't taken until 1990 mind your own business.

Harold turned back around and looked across the crater.

She was getting smaller. He thought if he was a scientist he would develop a drug so that when people walked away they wouldn't get smaller.

And it wouldn't hurt as much.

The cardinal that had flown over a little while ago landed on a rock about 20' to his right.

When he looked back way in the distance he saw the Lakota pulling Tinga up onto the back of the horse.

Now 40% of Harold wanted to wake up. But 60% wanted to see what would happen next.

Maybe there's another waitress on the moon.

The horse turned, they went away over the edge and were gone.

Harold heard a little clicking noise, he looked over and the bird appeared to be tap dancing.

He was looking up toward the sky and then down to his feet—up and down up and down.

He started making chirping noises and it seemed to Harold he began whistling the Beatles song "Helter Skelter."

"What a hard song to whistle," Harold thought.

The bird stopped what he was doing and looked over.

He somehow smiled a little bit and it looked like he had very little tiny teeth.

The boy thought the bird had nice bird teeth.

Harold looked way way past the bird and noticed after a couple of hundred yards everything was under a huge shadow.

The dark side of the moon.

He decided to go that way. Walking on and over and around rocks until he was in the shadow and he kept going. The bird walked with him.

It was dark but not pitch-dark. Everything looked like when you're on the earth and there's no moon.

He wanted to remember this thought so he wrote it down in his diary he was carrying in his dream. People keep dream diaries but this was different.

He continued walking along with his shoes crunching in the snow sounding moon dust.

Harold couldn't believe Tinga left with an Indian on a horse.

How could she just abruptly leave like that? He thought they were getting along just peachy.

Years later if a woman did that to him he would refer to it as "Meet an Indian."

Someone would say, "Hey what happened to that girl Ally you were seeing?"

"Oh she went to meet an Indian."

Maybe that's why she wanted to go over to the lake the whole time. That's a sneaky move.

"Well," he thought, "it just goes to show you that everyone is responsible for their own life."

As he walked on a tiny Chinese Zentis flew through the rectangle in his head.

This type of bird is about 3" long, it's blue and black and kind of looks like a cricket wearing a sweatshirt.

It only existed during the 276 years of the Ming Dynasty. They have red eyes like how people's eyes sometimes look in a photograph.

The thought the bird brought was how old will Elizabeth be when she first starts shaving her legs?

The crust of the dark side of the moon is three times as thick as the other side. Harold's source for this fact: reading in waiting room for sprained arm.

Harold learned a lot in doctor's office waiting rooms. He saw them as small one room universities. University of Waiting.

He didn't really feel the difference as he walked. The bird would walk a few feet then fly a few feet then walk again.

Walk, fly, walk, fly, walk, fly. Harold didn't know if the bird knew about the crust differences.

As they came to the top of a hill and looked down Harold was stunned to see that it was an enormous wide-open field of beautiful green grass.

Like the outfield at Fenway Park except about 6" thick and covered with yellow daffodils. And it went as far as he could see.

Way way in the distance was a banging metal sound. It

seemed to Harold to be the sound of a buoy. Definitely the air smelled faintly of salt.

He wasn't sure but he thought he again heard the sound of waves crashing very faintly. But he didn't see where it was coming from.

Harold and the bird stood there. He looked at the huge amount of stars in the distance.

The boy knew that some of the stars he was looking at had already burned out but that it took so long for the light to travel all that way they just appeared to still be there. Like some people.

He wondered if there was sound from the stars and that maybe someday all the sound that was coming from them would eventually be heard on the earth, coming an immeasurable amount of time after the light.

It would be a huge thunderous booming noise like a trillion atom bombs all at once.

The sound would be continuous nonstop for 850,000 years. Roughly.

All over the world people would be shitting themselves.

But maybe when God created everything, if there was a God, he made it so the stars had no sound on purpose because it would ruin the atmosphere of the galaxies.

Harold learned from his grandfather that light traveled faster than sound and once wrote a story about it in first grade.

The story was that the speed of sound and the speed of

light were camping out one night and they heard a noise in the woods. They thought that it might be a bear.

In front of them was a small fire making crackling noises. At the same time they decided to go see what it was.

As the speed of sound stood up to go the speed of light came back and said:

"It wasn't a bear it was a deer."

The speed of sound said:

"Oh."

And they both sat back down.

Even though the speed of light was the fastest thing in the universe he was a little bit insecure during the day because he felt like he was less appreciated.

The point Harold was making was that no matter what someone accomplished they still might not feel good enough.

Including God, if there was a God. Harold felt that even with everything he created and accomplished he must feel pretty bad with it all.

The consistent horror in the world.

And he deserved to feel bad. Very very bad.

His grandfather told him that the devil was God in a different mood.

They looked and listened to the fire. The speed of light joked that the light from the fire was reaching them before the crackling noises.

Kiddingly the speed of sound said to the speed of light:

"Go to hell, at least I can make noise."

"The only reason people give a shit about your noise is to see where I was."

Then they laughed and laughed and got stoned.

They were hysterically joking about how when people saw lightning they would count the seconds until they heard the thunder in order to determine how far away the lightning happened.

They thought it was hilarious because sometimes the thunder would wait longer on purpose just to screw with everyone.

In Harold's story the speed of light and the speed of sound fooled around like junior high school students.

Anthropomorphism was the longest word Harold could spell. In general he couldn't spell at all.

He memorized this word because he liked how long it was and he liked the meaning of it.

Which was: "The attribution of human traits and emotions to nonhuman entities." *Reader's Digest*—teeth cleaning—5 years old.

He thought maybe because he knew this word was the reason why a little while ago the bird seemed to be tap dancing and whistling "Helter Skelter."

As his grandfather once told him:

"Everything happens for a reason other than coincidences and most things."

Right after he said this he laughed uncontrollably and coughed for two minutes.

Even though Tinga was only gone for about 20 minutes Harold missed her. He wondered how far away she was.

Like counting the time between thunder and lightning.

He thought maybe that's what it is like when someone you love very much dies.

Harold random thought:

"His life will be declared a mistrial."

Chapter 10

Harold random thought:

A boy at Christmastime in the late 1800s being bad on purpose so Father Christmas would put coal in his stocking and that would help heat his family's house.

It was during one of Harold's visits to Maine while in the small motorboat crossing the lake that Harold's grandfather told him what the Lakota thought of thunder and lightning.

He said they believed in a Mythical bird called the Thunderbird and they believed when the bird flapped its wings that's what caused the thunder.

And the source of lightning was from the reflection of sunlight in the bird's eyes.

As he learned more about the scientific reason for things, he always liked the before science versions better.

Harold thought they somehow connected more to human beings even though they were mythical.

There was a beauty to it that science didn't have.

One time Ms. Yuka asked the class about thunder and lightning and Harold raised his hand and told her the Lakota version without saying it was from the Lakota.

Even though he knew the scientific version. He just wanted to see how Ms. Yuka would react.

She smiled and gently said in a way to not hurt Harold's feelings that that was some kind of fairy tale but was not the real reason.

She also said he had quite an imagination.

Harold thought of her tied to the stake surrounded by Lakota and a pack of growling wolves.

By the way the name of Harold's grandfather was Alexander.

A synthetic drawing of a beautiful bird that never existed glided through the rectangle.

Sleek and casual with crisp charcoal lines he flew. The closest looking to a real bird was a dove.

Perhaps a sociopath dove with violent tendencies. Perhaps a normal dove.

The thought the bird brought to Harold was to walk forward across the field of daffodils.

So he did. The cardinal walked beside him like a bird in a children's book.

He felt it was a very one-sided situation because the bird could go away from him way easier than he could go away from the bird.

Kind of like a bad marriage.

On and on they walked for about an hour. The grass slowly thinned out and then it was all sand. Beach sand.

They both stopped and about a hundred yards in the distance was what appeared to be an ocean.

Right before the water on the sand was a dark mass of something moving. About 8" or 10" tall.

The cardinal stood still. Harold squinted his 7 year old eyes to try and focus to that distance and could see that it was hundreds of birds.

He saw very far off to the right a higher piece of land or rock or cliff or something all in shadow.

At the top in silhouette appeared to be some kind of structure. Something that seemed to have been built.

Harold started walking straight ahead toward the water.

The sand was hard and a grey color like almost everything he'd seen on the moon.

It was the same color as the sand at Nahant Beach in Massachusetts where Harold had been many many times.

When he had walked about 50 yards the sand started to get a little bit wet. The birds were walking around like sandpipers. They didn't seem to notice Harold.

He decided to turn right and walk parallel to the birds and ocean toward the structure up on the hill in the distance. The cardinal walked beside him.

As he walked Harold began singing the song:

"Heigh-Ho, It's Off to Work We Go" from *Snow White and the Seven Dwarfs*.

The lyrics he sang were not the ones from the movie. They were ones he learned from his friends in the neighborhood. They were filthy.

It looked to Harold that the bird was blushing just from hearing the lyrics. He thought what a sissy this bird is.

The sound of the waves crashed. An unbelievable amount of stars. It seemed like two Milky Ways.

He saw what appeared to be double Big Dippers overlapping each other.

On and on he and the bird walked. To Harold the bird had a weird vibe. He just had a kind of intense energy about him.

Years later when Harold lived in New York City he would have a beautiful girlfriend that was also very very intense.

Her intenseness would make him tense. Very often he was weighing out if it was worth it.

One time in a fit of anger he said to her:

"You remind me of that fucking bird on the moon."

As they got closer to where they were headed he saw what seemed like a set of wooden stairs going up the steep side of rock. Looked like about 100' up to where the structure was.

From this distance it appeared to be a combination church/lighthouse. He was hesitant about going up.

The boy thought, "Why can't being on the moon be enough? Why do I have to go up the side of a cliff on some old wooden stairs on the dark side of the moon?"

A nocturnal parakeet addicted to barbiturates slowly drifted through the rectangle reminding Harold of the story his grandfather told him about taking risks.

It revolved around a 23 year young man from Holland named Anthony Fokker. He designed airplanes and worked for the Germans in WWI.

Anthony was the guy who figured out how the machine gun on the front of the plane could fire without hitting the propeller. He tested it himself.

Thinking about what Anthony had done Harold figured he could walk up a set of steps on the dark side of the moon in a dream.

He also thought he should name the cardinal Anthony Fokker in honor of what he had accomplished.

Briefly he imagined mounting a small machine gun on the bird's back just behind his head.

Harold approached the steps and stopped at the bottom.

It took 120 steps to the top.

As he ascended he ran the theme song to the movie *Summer of '42* three times in his head.

Arriving at the top he looked around.

The building was surrounded by 2' tall light green grass, the type that would be found in the dunes on Cape Cod, Massachusetts.

The structure was made of a combination of stone and wood. It was in fact a combination old church and lighthouse.

Rather than where the steeple would be there was a 35' tower and up at the top the light.

The side of the building facing him had 6 stained-glass windows shaped like 10' teardrops.

There were 2 paths through the grass. One went over to the building and looped around the rear of the church, probably to the back door.

The other went left toward the edge of the cliff. Harold went left and walked the 45' to the end. He looked out.

Way below waves were crashing onto huge rocks. It sounded fantastic. There's only one thing that sounded like that and that was it.

Like Louis Armstrong.

No seagulls were in sight. However all those birds on the beach were still down there off to the left, walking quickly all around like drug addicts.

Just then 3 small seagulls flew through the rectangle in his head laughing loudly and smelling of whiskey.

They brought 3 thoughts with them.

Number one was who would be his first real girlfriend and where was she right now? Besides Elizabeth of course.

She wasn't really his girlfriend other than in his head.

The second thought was would she break his heart or would he break hers?

Because being in love was like being on a seesaw where one side contained nitroglycerin.

When you first get on no one knows which side has it.

The third thought was that he remembered his grandfather told him that Winston Churchill hated pigeons.

After he died there was a statue of him built in the middle of London made of iron.

They put a small electrical current running through it so pigeons wouldn't land on and shit on him.

Harold thought he would like a small electrical current running through him now so no problems would land on him.

Maybe it would keep girls from hugging him and then he would never have a broken heart.

If some girl said, "Harold, I think you're cute."

He could say, "Tell that to Winston Churchill."

Looking out at the ocean Harold heard a single engine plane. But he saw no planes.

The ocean was lit up like there was a full moon. That made Harold laugh.

The waves were shimmering in the light. It looked like there were 3 million of those silver things used to pour gravy floating up and down as far as you could see.

Harold picked up a rock and threw it off the cliff as hard as he could but it didn't reach the water.

There he stood on the dark side of the moon looking out at the ocean. The side he was on faced the opposite direction of the earth.

He was all alone and still he was not lonely.

He noticed off to his left the cardinal was standing there watching him.

Harold didn't see him climb the steps so he figured he must have flown up.

Harold thought that God made the bird, if there was a God, and Elizabeth and Ms. Yuka and the Lakota and the earth and the moon and his mind and Tinga and this dream and his grandfather and Moosehead Lake.

Even though God made all those things, if there was a God, Harold took full responsibility for what he did next:

To amuse himself he began fake tap dancing and singing

"Moon River" very slow and deep like a record being played at the wrong speed.

He danced as fast he could back down the path all the way to where it connected to the other path and continued all the way around to the back door of the building where he stopped. No more dancing no more singing.

The bird had walked quickly along beside him and then also stopped.

Harold tried to dance like Gene Kelly and Fred Astaire but in his mind he imagined that he was one guy with both their heads.

He actually had no idea how to dance.

Incidentally Harold never liked Gene Kelly and Fred Astaire because he really disliked that type of dancing even though he knew it was probably very difficult.

The clothes they both wore in those movies also irritated him and pissed him off.

They were too silky and shiny and colorful and baggy.

He was exhausted from what he just did and he wasn't even really dancing.

Harold and Anthony stood at the bottom of the three steps that went up to the door of the building.

There was no door where a door would be.

He looked over to his right and about 30' away in the tall grass there were some old crooked gravestones. Resembling ones from the 1700s–1800s. Harold walked over to see them.

There were about 25 of them and they all had the same thing carved on them—

He came back to the building and thought of killing and eating Anthony but changed his mind for several reasons.

Harold walked up the 3 steps and into the building.

The inside was a huge open room with extremely high cathedral ceilings. It was completely empty except for a podium and one old wooden pew that would seat about 7 people.

The podium was off to the left facing the room. Standing on the front edge was what appeared to be a bluebird wearing a green leather vest.

The pew was about halfway into the room facing forward.

Harold stood still and noticed in the front right corner a spiral staircase that went up into darkness. Probably up to where the lighthouse light was.

Anthony walked in and stood beside Harold. The two birds made eye contact and Anthony started growling like a German shepherd.

Just like the dogs the Nazis had all through the war. The Nazis were a perfect example that maybe there is no God.

And if there really is a God and then there's the Nazis, you have to think about God:

"What the fuck?"

The bird at the podium had no reaction to Anthony in a way that was somehow laughing at him.

Like a comedian ignoring a heckler.

Harold thought of killing both of the birds, with no intention of eating them, but changed his mind for several reasons.

He thought that he might be having such violent thoughts because of the history of the Catholic Church and all other religions.

Harold walked into the room going toward the staircase. The floors were 10" wide dark blond wooden planks.

As he walked, the bird at the podium watched him. Anthony didn't move.

Harold got to the bottom of the staircase and looked up. It was made of grey black steel and went up higher and higher into darkness.

He thought he would climb these stairs but not right now. Instead he walked back to the pew and sat down. Anthony walked over and stood on the floor beside the pew.

The bird standing at the podium began speaking English in a thick Italian accent.

Although this was not a movie, Harold thought the bird could easily have been speaking Italian with live English subtitles, but he wasn't. Live subtitles.

One of the things the bird said was that all birds could talk but God made it so people would only hear it when parrots talked so that they would think they were the only birds that could speak.

He said God did this just to amuse himself. Harold knew that dreams were based on reactions to what happened in one's life but he could not—no matter how hard he tried—figure out what would have contributed to this bird talking in this church.

He looked like he was wearing sunglasses but he wasn't.

The bird was difficult to understand so Harold wasn't sure if he was hearing him correctly.

At one point he thought he was comparing a young Brigitte Bardot to a young Julie Christie and said something about God made both of them and that they were both by far better than the Big Dipper.

Harold then remembered that he had seen two Big Dippers in the sky and wondered if there was a connection.

It was funny to him that he had never done any drugs in his life and this was a dream he was having. What would his dreams be like if he was on drugs?

The bird continued talking and seemed to be gesturing with his right wing to one of the stained glass windows. Harold and Anthony looked over.

He wasn't sure but he thought the bird was saying that the guy who invented stained glass windows was the same guy that also invented the kaleidoscope. He seemed to be insinuating that religion and the children's toy were similar in that they were both invented to distract and entertain.

The bird was now mumbling and started flipping through some papers on the podium that Harold hadn't noticed before.

Harold looked over at Anthony who stood on the floor and was now wearing blue and white spats.

It was from out of the mouth of this bird at the podium that Harold first heard the sentence that he would end up saying to many people over the course of his lifetime—

"Jesus loves you because he doesn't know you."

The ocean was heard through the open windows in the wall 20' behind the bird. Through these windows Harold started to notice some stars.

The bird wasn't really saying a mass so Harold assumed there would be no communion.

Which was good because he hadn't gone to confession since he had received his first Holy Communion several months earlier. And even then he didn't really confess to anything.

At his first confession he had an argument with the priest over all the wars fought in the name of the church and that the idea of confessing his sins to him would be like apologizing to the devil over stealing a cupcake.

An Arabian Tin Hawk with silver tipped wings glided through the rectangle inside Harold's head humming "Take Me Out to the Ball Game."

These birds were addicted to odd numbers and were never seen in pairs or any combination of even numbers. This bird brought no thought, very rare.

Remembering this entire dream was causing Harold to miss being in the class.

He wondered if this was what it was like when you're dead. A very very long dream that you never wake up from.

A dream that you had when you were alive.

The bird at the podium stopped talking, paused for a moment and then began singing "Spanish Eyes" by Al Martino.

Harold wasn't sure at first but then he realized that Anthony was quietly singing along.

He assumed the bird was a fan of Al Martino because they were both Italian but he didn't really know.

Just then it started pouring rain. It looked great out the windows behind the bird. And the sound of it hitting the roof was fantastic. It was one of Harold's favorite sounds.

It made him think of Moosehead Lake and his bedroom on the third floor with the ceilings at an angle.

Sometimes when it rained hard he would get out of his bed and look out the window.

He loved seeing the rain hitting the leaves on the trees.

And when the drops hit the lake it looked a temporary circle ballet.

Harold stood up, took a few steps to his right and said excuse me to Anthony, then he knelt down and did the sign of the cross.

He stood back up and walked down the aisle past the podium to the back wall of the church and looked out the window on the right.

Although it was pouring rain the ocean still had that lit up look like a full moon. Harold smiled. It was breathtaking. He heard the sound of the waves crashing 100' below.

The birds continued singing "Spanish Eyes" and the wide-open high ceilinged wooden and stone building gave it a nice gentle reverb.

He turned around to take it all in. The stained glass windows were beautiful and Anthony stood in same spot singing along.

Harold thought his blue and white spats looked ridiculous but he would never say it because he could tell Anthony really liked them and he wouldn't want to hurt his feelings.

It was at this point that Harold once again thought that he might be insane.

If he was he wanted to be fully insane because he thought that people who were temporarily insane were sissies. Like his mother.

Harold turned around and looked back out the window.

Suddenly it began to thunder and lightning inside his head. He didn't have to count the delay because it was at the exact same time.

Then the rain outside stopped. He thought it was going to start raining inside his head but it didn't.

What surprised him most about this was that he never got headaches and even now he still did not get one.

He looked down the beach way off to the left and saw that those hundreds of birds were still there.

There was another thunder and lightning in his head that seemed to startle those birds and they all flew up and off to the left turning all at once and going higher and out over the ocean and out of sight.

Then it began snowing heavily in his head. A blizzard.

Very windy but he could still hear in the background the birds singing "Spanish Eyes" by Al Martino.

A small drive-in theater appeared in his head. Playing on the screen was news footage from WWII.

An update about Rommel fighting Montgomery in North Africa.

Through the snow there were many images of tanks in the desert. Somehow beautiful and surreal and horrible.

Harold read in *Reader's Digest* that the sons of both men became great friends years after the war as adults.

To him this somehow magnified the insanity and ridiculousness of war.

Then it all stopped and his head was back to normal. Ha, normal.

The birds finished singing "Spanish Eyes" by Al Martino.

He heard some rustling of papers and the Italian bird at the podium said something that could not be understood and then began singing: "Hey, Good Lookin'" by Hank Williams. Anthony was singing harmony.

Harold thought that Emmylou Harris would fit nicely with them as he looked to his right at the spiral staircase.

Chapter 11

On his way up his footsteps echoed off the stone walls and the steel spiral staircase. Harold thought that an echo was audio plagiarism.

As he went higher it got darker because there were no windows along the way.

The tide continued to go out.

He remembered his grandfather telling him that there is no time and time is moving slow and fast all at once. He continued:

"A snail is taking tiny tiny steps on the armrest of a seat. A seat that's on a 747, cruise speed 580. Or the Concorde, cruise speed 1,356 miles per hour.

"That's your life. You're a snail on a jet."

He said some people don't respect the little time they have and waste it. A lot of it.

Throwing their time into a wood chipper.

They also destroy other people's time by being upset over meaningless fucking bullshit.

Harold's mother did this all the time.

He kept climbing.

At the top was a large round room that housed the giant light.

All the way around 12 large windows made it look like a greenhouse. The light was not on.

He wondered if the number of windows had anything to do with the apostles.

The floor of the room was made of thick stone. One of the panes of glass had a glass door within it that went out to a balcony.

He walked out over to the 4' high railing.

As the ocean kept taking steps backwards Harold saw something being revealed in the sand.

Little structures. 1' tall lighthouses. Perfect size for a birdhouse. Birdhouse lighthouses.

Some had lights beaming out and going around.

Different ones had different colored lights, green, yellow, blue, violet sweeping around.

His grandfather would love to be seeing what he was seeing.

Harold promised himself he would do a painting of this and give it to his grandfather.

He could put it on one of the hooks on the wall in the house in Maine.

First he thought he would show the painting in Ms. Yuka's class to get extra credit.

Ms. Yuka might say—"Could you explain this painting, Harold?"

"Yes this a painting of the ocean on the dark side of the moon as seen from the top of a lighthouse.

"When the tide goes way out these 100 little combination lighthouse birdhouses are revealed. That's it."

"I see, that's a very interesting idea."

"It's not an idea, it's it."

"Well I really like it."

Around and around went the colored lights. They looked like miniature Aurora Borealises.

Harold's grandfather told him that the Lakota saw the Northern Lights as the spirit of children that had been born dead.

He thought that was very sad on one hand but on the other hand it was a celebration of the little babies which was beautiful.

Like the fireworks at the cemetery on the hill.

This interpretation reminded Harold of a black and white photograph his grandfather once showed him of the Lakota Sioux elder Benjamin Black Elk standing in the Black Hills of South Dakota in front of Mount Rushmore.

Here are these huge magnificent sculptures of the people who represent freedom and independence.

Perhaps:

"Mount Hypocrite."

The 7 year old was learning that the bullshit was all around. Politics, religion, his mother, the world.

If Harold ever prayed to God, if there was a God, one of

the things he hoped for was that no contradicting information would ever come out about Jesus.

Just so there would be at least one person not ruined by shrapnel coming from the bomb of truth.

When he was actually having the dream (as opposed to running it through his mind in the class) he remembered that at this point he began to feel homesick even though he knew he was asleep in his own bed.

Then he thought that being asleep and dreaming was like being in two places at the same time.

He had to remember to bring this up to Ms. Yuka because she casually once said that was impossible.

As he stood at the railing he noticed a flock of birds flying from left to right. Maybe about 15 of them.

They descended beautifully landing on the beach in the area of the lighthouses.

Harold watched them casually walking around on the wet sand.

They looked like crows except they were dark green and wearing silver eyeliner.

The birds started moving in a more purposeful way. Each one moving toward the bird lighthouses and then stepping in.

He watched as all the lights kept going around. Harold thought the birds were maybe going to shut the lights off but they didn't.

The tide was going further out but slower now.

A bird made of red petrified sprouts went through the rectangle and seemed to be mumbling something about Claude Rains.

This bird brought the thought to Harold of the first time he ever saw a bird.

He was about 11 months old holding on to the windowsill with his little fingers. Leaning his head back for maximum viewing.

It was snowing. He thought the sky broke.

Harold was glad he couldn't talk because it gave him more privacy. But he certainly could think.

Suddenly a bright red bird landed on the branch of a maple tree right out the window.

The image looked black and white except for the bird.

He thought what an odd animal, if it is an animal. What is this thing moving in such a jerky manner.

The bird was standing with his back to Harold then suddenly whipped around and was now looking right at him. They stared at each other.

The bird felt bad for Harold because he knew he couldn't fly. He'd seen people before.

He could also tell that Harold was not in charge of his own life at all just from looking at him for 10 seconds.

The bird didn't know what a second was and neither did Harold.

It would take Harold 5 more years to learn what a second was. By then the bird would have died a long time ago.

This red animal had skinny twiglike legs. The knees were on the back. Fascinating.

Years later in Ms. Yuka's class he would notice this again

thinking it was for the first time. Not remembering he noticed it already as a baby type person.

Harold's own legs were fat and pinkish white. He liked the bird's legs better.

Although it was impossible the bird smiled and winked at Harold.

How could he know at this time that he might indeed be a little bit insane. You might say a dusting. Like the amount of snow on the driveway that cannot even be measured in depth.

He did not know that he would love these creatures for the rest of his life.

In Ms. Yuka's class Harold learned that birds went back to the time of dinosaurs.

He wondered if there could be one bird that was still alive since then that nobody knew about.

He knew this could not really be possible but he also knew the definition of *suspended disbelief.*

Which was "the willingness to suspend one's critical facilities and believe the unbelievable; sacrifice of realism and logic for the sake of enjoyment."

15 years after Ms. Yuka's class, at the age of 22, after drinking in a bar near the Naval Base in San Diego Harold almost had this definition tattooed on his balls.

Sometimes he would look at a bird and softly say out loud:

"I know it's you. Happy 230 millionth birthday my friend."

He once said this to a parakeet his aunt had in a cage in

her living room and he didn't realize she was standing in the doorway watching him. Then he heard:

"Hi Harold."

Slowly he turned around without moving.

"Hi Auntie. By the way how long have you had this bird?"

"Jenny is 2 years old."

Harold looked at her and in his mind he said:

"That's what you think."

Then he started to do a soft fake tap dance like in the old movies.

She watched him and smiled.

Harold stood at the railing, closed his 7 year old eyes and listened to the sounds.

He thought if his eyes were shut and therefore less information was going into his head that he wouldn't be thinking as much but it didn't work.

He heard children playing on the beach in the distance. There was the sound of screams mixed in with the waves smashing.

Even though he was only 7 he and everyone in the world learns the difference between happy playing screams and danger screams.

Harold loved seeing so much and appreciated it so much that sometimes if he woke up in the middle of the night and opened his eyes and saw total blackness he would be so afraid that he had lost his sight that he would jump out of the bed and run over to the window and look outside to make sure he could still see.

He did not have the patience yet to wait for his eyes to adjust to the darkness of the room.

Even though his eyes were shut he could still see, he could see things on the inside of his head.

Harold was happy and grateful and appreciated that he had sight and could walk around and witness the earth.

He wished that there was some way a boy could have two childhoods.

Then he thought everyone really does have two child-hoods in a way—if you divide the consciousness and the sub-conscious.

Inside Harold's head very very far in the distance there were two shiny black and yellow birds approaching the rectangle quickly.

The thought the first bird brought was that it would have been better if evolution had worked backwards.

Started out with man and then evolved into apes because there would be no more large-scale wars.

No more weapons made out of metal for the purpose of shredding human beings.

Instead a couple of fights in trees and caves with rocks and clubs over food and women.

The second bird had bright white eyes that made him look insane. He was insane. He also had a crush on Walt Disney.

Walt Disney drove this bird wild.

This bird caused Harold to wonder why time was always measured forward and backward but never off to the side. It seemed so simple.

There's always north, south, east and west so why not that with time?

In fact he thought he should write an essay on that for Ms. Yuka's class:

"The Peripheral World of Time by Harold the Magic Boy."

He figured this essay would come with a soundtrack which would be the sound of waves crashing. It would automatically play the length of time it took the reader to read it.

Harold realized that music of any kind changed the situation. He thought stamps should have music. Very short 2-second soundtracks.

It certainly was very quiet up there at the top of the lighthouse.

It reminded him of Cape Cod a few weeks after Labor Day.

He loved Massachusetts.

Harold then opened his eyes, stood at the railing for a few seconds looking at the two Big Dippers and two Little Dippers then abruptly went back down the spiral staircase and outside the lighthouse over to the edge of the cliff then down the 120 wooden steps to the beach.

If Anthony and the priest bird were still there he didn't notice.

He then walked out on the beach. The lights on the little lighthouse birdhouses were still going around and around.

He thought he could see silhouettes of some birds in the windows.

Briefly he wondered who the first guy was who ever saw a silhouette and how he reacted. He imagined him going back into the cave and saying:

"I just saw a two-dimensional guy that might have been naked, I'm not sure I couldn't really tell."

Harold squatted down and with his hands started to dig a hole, making an Adirondack chair.

The sand on this beach on the dark side of the moon was different than earth beach sand. It seemed to be like hourglass sand.

It very well may have been.

Harold thought how extraordinarily exciting it would be to play in a sandbox filled with hourglass sand.

Chapter 12

Sitting in his new chair made of a hole in the sand Harold looked back up at the sky.

The sky had twice as many stars as the earth's stars.

He thought of something Tinga said, which was—"The universe is underrated."

He smiled and agreed.

Harold wondered where Anthony was. He thought he sang excellent harmony.

In his opinion, although very intense, he thought Anthony was good people even though he was a bird.

Staring up at the huge amount of stars he thought back to the first time he went to the planetarium.

He remembered wanting to ask the man explaining the sky if all the stars that could be seen by the naked eye were all lined up in a straight row how many miles did he think they would go?

But he didn't ask him because Harold had a feeling he didn't even know where the bathrooms were.

It occurred to him that he hadn't really seen the sun during this entire dream although everything was kind of lit up like a full moon.

Even the dark side which he was now on was not in total darkness.

He remembered reading in a *Reader's Digest* magazine that the sun was one continuous nuclear explosion that had been going on for 4.5 billion years.

Sometimes to amuse himself Harold thought of the sun as a very large case of arson.

Now for some reason the view of the stars he was looking at reminded him of the stars over Moosehead Lake this past summer. He was staying with his grandfather in August.

Harold and his grandfather were at the very top room of the lake house which was actually a workshop full of the usual tools for absolutely everything.

His grandfather Alexander was one of those guys that could fix anything and build anything. Harold would never be one of those guys.

The room was a cupola type structure except that it wasn't round it was square. It smelled of oil and sawdust and kerosene and lilacs.

Hanging down one of the walls was a brass telescope like in the pirate movies. It had a piece of rawhide at the small end that hung on a wooden hook.

Alexander took the telescope off the wall and handed it

to Harold and said, "Look out this window straight across the lake."

So he did.

He was barely tall enough to see out.

People said Harold was small for his age which pissed him off and made no sense to him because this was his age and this was his height and weight and one thing he knew about, even at 7 years old, was that you couldn't argue with math.

To him the concept of comparing him to the general size of other children was like comparing a glass of water to the Indian Ocean and saying that one of them was wrong.

So Harold looked through the telescope across the lake.

"Do you see the only light there, that yellowish light that's down near the water on the other side?"

This was about half a mile away.

"Yes," said Harold whose middle name incidentally was Alexander.

"Yes, I see it."

"Well, today is Friday and Sunday you and I are going over there to go to a wedding."

"Oh ok."

Harold had never been to a wedding before. He sat in the front of the 15' motorboat. His grandfather sat in the back with his hand on the throttle of the 1959 35 horsepower Evinrude outboard engine.

It was about 9 a.m. and every time they headed out to cross the lake it was amazing and magical to Harold.

He sat facing the back of the boat watching the dock and

the rocky shore and the very tall thick balsam fir and pine trees quickly getting smaller.

The sound the engine made and the smell of the exhaust were burned into his mind.

For the rest of his life that smell would instantly bring him back to being on the lake in Maine.

He would realize that the sense of smell somehow had a more powerful connection with the memory. Why, he did not know.

Probably another thing God pulled for some reason, if there was a God.

The huge 3-story house with its weathered dark brown almost blackened shingles and painted dark green trim was also getting very little and fading behind the trees.

Even though they were traveling horizontally across the huge cold lake, Harold always liked to imagine that they were in some kind of spaceship going straight up into the sky.

However long they were traveling in the boat would be how long they were going up vertically at the same speed.

He liked to think that where they ended up on the other side of the lake was as different to him as if they had gone to another planet.

Especially that day going to a wedding.

Years later, as an adult, he would also think the same thing as he took the ferry from the coast of Rhode Island.

Usually they crossed to go to the only town on the lake which was Greenville.

That was where the store was where Harold would fake shoplift.

Where they were going this time was not as far as the town, it was about a 30 minute ride in the boat.

The people getting married were friends of Harold's grandfather.

The groom, Warren, was 79 years old, and Helen, the bride, was 78. It was his first marriage and her second.

He would joke to people that the reason he was getting married at that age was that it took him that long to find a virgin.

Harold's grandfather wanted him to be dressed very nicely for the wedding but none of his clothes were for such an occasion.

He had one pair of black corduroy pants that were now grey from being washed so many times and 3 long sleeved shirts.

He only wore long sleeved shirts even in the summer because he didn't like the feeling of his bare elbows touching things.

Harold did not know that this was something he had in common with Howard Hughes.

However a few days before the wedding Harold's grandfather knew that down underneath the house, where the rowboats were kept along with other random things, there might be an answer to the boy's clothes dilemma.

They both went down to look around. There on the left tossed carelessly on top of a pile of oars was a 4'1" marionette with the strings still attached to the wooden control cross.

Harold faced his grandfather in the boat and liked that they were both wearing western-style ties with their suits.

The kind like the gamblers wore in the movies.

On the seat between them was an oak box wrapped in tinfoil which contained the wedding gifts.

Three books, *Oliver Twist* and *A Tale of Two Cities*, both autographed by Charles Dickens.

Also in the box was a Bible autographed by Jesus, but that was just to be funny. And a small 8' canoe made of dark brown bark.

It was a Lakota child's toy that his grandfather had for many many years.

As Harold sat on the moon looking up at the stars he remembered how he loved wearing his red and black checkered marionette suit made of some kind of smooth thick fabric and how it kept him warm as they whipped across the lake that morning.

He didn't mind that it was about one size too small. His grandfather's was dark blue, they both wore white shirts.

He also loved that the label inside said MADE IN LONDON.

People at the wedding probably thought that Harold was a shy boy but he wasn't, he just didn't feel like talking to people.

They walked up the hill to the farmhouse with no farm in sight.

To the left of the house on the lawn were several long tables surrounded by chairs for lots and lots of people, there stood about eight people mingling. Harold and his grandfather were early.

His grandfather was always early which was a trait that Harold would pick up 50 years later.

Sometimes jokingly he would say to Harold:

"If we leave now we'll have just enough time to be late."

They went in the side door of the house opposite the gathering into the kitchen where there was coffee.

First they toasted.

"Here's to toasting," which was what they always did no matter what they were drinking.

Framed on one of the kitchen walls was an 8" by 10" off-white piece of paper with something written on it in black India ink.

Harold walked over to look at it.

It said:

Warren Barnlett—date of birth 1884—died—not yet.
Time wasted—approximately 20 years.

The last sentence at the bottom said:

preliminary gravestone information

At dusk Harold was standing away from the winding-down celebration staring at the sky over the lake watching the slow appearance of the stars.

It seemed as if when each guest left another star arrived.

He wasn't thinking about earlier in the day when some of the women were asking him to go over there and get that and go over there and bring them this.

He would just do it. He was not bothered by the 2" or 3" strings that hung from the key parts of his marionette suit, because when his grandfather cut them to release it from the wooden control he did it very casually.

His grandfather saw from a distance what the women had him doing and watched for a little while.

Then he motioned for Harold to come over, leaned down to him and quietly and privately said:

"Listen to me—don't ever do what a woman tells you to do."

This statement was burned into his head as if his brain had been branded.

There were many people at the wedding. A sunny summer day in August. Harold and his grandfather walked all around sometimes together sometimes separately.

The 6' tall man towering over his little grandson. He was very warm and friendly and would say many things to people. Sometimes funny things.

However Harold noticed something else about him—he would ask people questions and he listened a lot. He was a very good listener.

He wouldn't cut in and say something and cut the person off.

One reason Harold noticed this was because he loved math and he sometimes liked to measure random things because he found it very interesting.

He became aware of it in Ms. Yuka's class watching her in charge. He figured she did 98% of the talking which to him indicated a dictatorship.

Intellectually he knew it was an elementary school class so that's just how it was but from another angle (like the spokes on a wheel) he thought it was truly unfair.

To him just because she had been around longer didn't mean she was more important. That's why people bought new cars.

Even years later Harold would notice in conversations if it was a balance, a back-and-forth like a tennis match, or if someone selfishly dominated. A time whore.

In Ms. Yuka's class he once wrote a poem about it called:
"Listen"
The last lines were—

I know you know you do it,
it doesn't matter to you at all
you just want to keep on
    talking
a verbal waterfall.

At the wedding Warren took Harold and his grandfather out to the old barn, which was about 30 yards to the left of the house.

They walked up the stairs to a loft type area that Warren used to paint in.

He had removed a lot of the wall and replaced it with big windows that faced the lake.

On a tripod was a nice 4' long telescope that Warren bought at Sears in 1961.

The three of them took turns looking through it. Harold looked through it pointing it back to their own house. In the trees were lots and lots of birds.

Chapter 13

Harold wondered why when you look through the telescope you see everything inside a circle but when you just look out your own eyes there's no circles.

He figured it must be another God shenanigan, if there is a God.

Warren motioned with his hand to the walls and shelves.

There were many many paintings of beautiful birds. The place was full of them.

Harold noticed this when he first walked into the loft because he noticed everything.

He was also very aware of the smell of turpentine and paint and liked it immediately in the same way that he liked the smell of nail polish remover.

He also loved the smell of oil when the oilman would come to his house to fill the tank.

The tank was in the basement and the guy would back down the driveway and attach a hose from the truck to the pipe on the side of the house.

Harold would stand in the driveway and watch the man

do this while inhaling the smell that he loved that Ms. Yuka said was from dead dinosaurs.

When she told this to the class Harold had three quick thoughts—first could Ms. Yuka possibly have escaped from an insane asylum?

And second—if he liked the smell of oil would he also like the smell of a live dinosaur?

Which made him think of another thing—that nobody, not even fancy scientists, knew what a live dinosaur smelled like.

They could have all their bullshit theories and bullshit guesses but they would NEVER EVER REALLY KNOW!!!

All of that went through Harold's head in a half second like three birds flying through the rectangle.

The paintings were many different sizes and the colors were very crisp.

Most of them were on white backgrounds, not in trees or in the sky or walking on the beach.

There was one of a bird in a cage.

Harold wondered how Warren could paint a bird so well because a bird never stopped moving. Which made him think when does a bird sleep?

He'd never seen a sleeping bird.

He made a mental note in his head to write that down:

I've never seen a sleeping bird.

Harold asked Warren:

"How do you paint the birds so well if they never stop moving?"

"Very interesting question Harold, nobody's ever asked me that before.

"When I think of the bird I can have him not move in my mind, so I look at it really and then in my mind—back and forth.

"Sometimes the image of a bird can stay in my head for years and years so I can still see him without really looking at him.

"It's kind of like painting fire."

"Do you ever just make up a bird in your mind that doesn't even really exist?

"Make up what he looks like and what the bird is called and his behavior and everything?"

Smiling, Warren said:

"No Harold, I've never even thought of that but maybe I should try it. No I have to paint real birds because I paint for the Peterson's bird guide books."

Warren turned around to one of the shelves, picked up a book and handed it to Harold.

"You can have it if you want."

He took it in his little boy hands.

"Thank you very much."

His grandfather watched and smiled and Harold would never know that he loved seeing this moment.

It was a paperback with a light green cover about 6" long, 4" wide and 2" thick.

On the cover was a painting of an American Eagle in the middle, the Bald Eagle.

With a bluebird to its left and a cardinal to its right.

Harold looked at them intently.

"How did you paint them so small?"

"I didn't, the people who made the book photographed the paintings and then shrunk them down so they would all fit in."

Harold wondered if that's what happened to his cock.

He also wondered how big the book would be if all the pictures were the size of the original paintings.

He figured it would have to be about the size of a shed.

Of the 5 empty bedrooms at his grandfather's huge old wooden house he could chose from, Harold chose the one that was closest to the peak on the 3rd floor.

He liked that the thick wooden ceiling was on an angle. It made the room more interesting to him.

It had one window in the A shape of the wall facing the lake.

The smell of the wood was all around him.

It was a single bed with a black iron frame. When he was in it his head was near the opposite wall which allowed him to see out.

That night he was lying under the covers with the lamp on looking at the bird book.

After a while he imagined that he was a bird inside a birdhouse.

As a bird he imagined that he was resting having flown the 1400 mile round trip from Halifax, Nova Scotia, out to the site of the sinking of the *Titanic* and back.

He just wanted to see it.

He wondered if there had been any birds in cages on the *Titanic* that weren't let out before it sank because they were lost in the commotion.

He was curious if when birds see each other do they ask in their bird language:

"How was your flight?"

Just to be sarcastic.

Harold thought of all the animals in the world to be put into a cage it had to be worse for a bird because of the difference of where he could go before.

He also thought it would be horrible for any animal.

He even thought it was worse for animals than it was for people who were put in jail because the animals didn't commit a crime. They were put in there just so humans could look at them.

That in itself could be seen as a crime.

He spent a long time looking at the little paintings and reading about the birds in the book.

There were about 7 birds on each page and the book was 120 pages long. He had no idea there were that many birds in the world.

Just then a sparrow landed on the windowsill giving Harold a left profile.

He then slowly turned his head looking right at the boy. The bird began mouthing the words:

"Too bad you can't fly."

Harold gave him the finger and he flew away.

He thought of a sissy bird that was afraid of heights.

A very violent looking sparrow flew through the rectangle.

It brought one of the weirdest paranoid thoughts Harold had ever had which was that he had to remember tomorrow to tell his grandfather that if he himself died unexpectedly he did not want to be buried in the marionette suit.

The suit was hanging in his bedroom closet.

Harold continued to look out the window with his head lying comfortably on the soft flannel red and green sheets that had the repeated image of a bird hunter with his dog.

He thought what if rather than flying south and then landing somewhere the birds just kept going.

They kept going straight out of the earth's atmosphere into outer space.

Every bird in the world, there were no more birds left.

"Into Outer Space."

He had to remember to write that sentence down.

Although sleepy a fantastic idea occurred to him—he should make his own book of completely made-up birds.

He put his feet into his little moccasins, walked over to his wicker suitcase and got his red notebook.

Jumped back in bed and began drawing little birds as accurately as he could based on his imagination.

What a magical day this was, going to the wedding and Warren giving him the bird book.

Harold sat on the moon and tried not to think. He was exhausted from thinking. He tried to not think but he couldn't do it.

He leaned back in his Adirondack chair made of sand looking at the live painting of the stars and outer space.

He saw what was really happening as a live painting.

Chapter 14

Now he missed Elizabeth. He had the brief thought of waking up from this dream on the moon but then decided not to. He wanted more of it.

Besides Elizabeth would always be in the class but he wouldn't always be on the moon.

Watching the earth 238,900 miles in the distance he wondered how many appointments people had to go to on this one day.

A Jamaican Eagle flew through the rectangle causing Harold to wonder who the first guy was in the world that had an appointment. And what was it for.

He considered shooting the next bird to fly through the rectangle because he was fed up with thinking so much.

The boy was begging not to think. He knew the only way was to be asleep without dreaming.

In regards to not thinking he saw himself as a failure.

Here's an example of not being able to stop thinking:

He remembered his grandfather had a 14" by 18" photograph of a mirror on the wall in his house so that when he looked in it there would be no reflection.

He did this for two reasons. One, for more privacy and two because he thought it was funny.

Harold remembered when he borrowed the photograph of the mirror and brought it into show-and-tell.

He stood at the front of the class and held it up facing the students and Ms. Yuka who was standing at the back.

Harold said:

"This is a photograph of a mirror and its purpose is to have no reflection for more privacy and to be funny. Are there any questions?"

Total silence, then Pamela Clancy raised her hand and asked:

"Have you ever held that up to a real mirror just for the surrealism of it?"

She was 8.

"No I haven't but what a very interesting idea. I must try that."

Then he sat down.

Ms. Yuka had a small smile. Nobody knew that she wasn't really focused because she was so incredibly horny.

That's just what happens when women are in their late 20s early 30s.

Now the sound of a breeze traveled through Harold's mind as he sat on the moon.

He noticed an Italian Sea Sparrow gliding through the rectangle.

This bird would have landed on the windowsill of Leonardo da Vinci's studio and distracted him, where he did the drawings of his inventions of helicopters, submarines, and flying machines, but it didn't because it didn't exist then and was created 5 centuries later in the mind of a 7 year old boy during his very long dream.

This bird reminded Harold of another time he was visiting his grandfather in Maine.

They were outside one summer night at the fire pit that was halfway between the house and lake.

In the fire pit about to be lit were several pieces of split wood.

The thing about this fire was that underneath the wood, to be used as kindling, were player piano paper rolls of songs. 3 of them.

Each one was about the size of a Maxwell House coffee can.

Harold's grandfather hated these songs. He bought them at a yard sale.

Harold could only remember the name of one of the songs which was "Happy Days Are Here Again."

His grandfather did not have a player piano.

He remembered him saying:

"You can't really burn the sound of a song but this is the next best thing."

Then he laughed madly.

Later as they sat at the fire his grandfather started whistling "Happy Days Are Here Again." Which was confusing to Harold.

He wondered why someone would whistle a song they didn't like?

Then he thought it was better than not being able to whistle a song that you did like.

Sometimes Harold wondered why he was alive. He couldn't think of a real reason. This thought was brought to him on his own.

There were no birds involved.

He wondered if birds thought about why they were alive.

Harold once got a piece of paper and a pencil and he tried to make a list of the reasons why. He didn't write anything.

It seemed to him the problem was he was smart enough to ask the question but not smart enough to answer it.

Then he thought maybe that goes for the entire human race.

Maybe that was another shenanigan God did, if there is a God.

He's sitting there thinking:

"I know, I'll have them all wonder about this enormous situation but not be able to answer it! Yes! That's hilarious!!! Hahaha!!!"

That same night at the fire pit he said to his grandfather:

"Why is everyone alive?"

He waited and watched as his grandfather stared into the fire.

Then without looking at Harold he said:

"It's just for something to do." Then he started laughing.

He continued:

"I'm laughing because that's the biggest question in the whole world and it's so big I can't answer it and no one can answer it.

"It might have to do with God—if there is a God."

"You mean maybe there is no God?"

"Yes that's correct—maybe there is no God. But don't worry about it, there's no sense in that.

"Even if there is no God that won't change anything."

Then he laughed a little bit more.

Many many years later one of the most important people in Harold's life would tell him the purpose of life was to enjoy your life. Peter was his name.

Harold stopped thinking about his dream on the moon and sat in the present.

He looked down at his hands that he laid flat on his desk.

They were the hands of an old man. Deep wrinkles in them. Attached to his young wrists, it appeared they were from another person.

Harold knew they looked just like his grandfather's hands and that made him happy.

His grandfather was his favorite person in the whole world.

He even thought he saw him during the dream on the moon, standing over near the birdhouse that was on the pole near the outdoor cafe.

Harold picked up a green crayon that was on his desk and held it up to his nose and looked at Ms. Yuka who was at the front of the class talking about something.

He smelled the crayon and looked at her so it seemed that she smelled like a green crayon.

He wasn't sure why he was doing this but he was very amused by it and kept sniffing and sniffing.

She was explaining something to the class about the planet Neptune.

Then she said:

"Harold, do you have something to say?"

Now he thought, "God, if there is a God, please give me something."

Just in the nick of time a miniature Gold Colored Vulture only found in Himalayan fairy tales whipped through the rectangle and brought to Harold the thought of what to say to the beautiful plain looking Ms. Yuka.

"Yes Ms. Yuka, I would like to ask you why are all the planets round instead of other shapes?"

Harold knew the answer to this question because his sister was having a problem with one of her baby teeth. It was going sideways and wasn't coming out.

Ironically their dentist's name was Dr. Christmas. A God shenanigan.

The answer was because of gravity, the planets, not her tooth.

"Well Harold, it's because gravity is pulling the planet to the center. It pulls from the center to the outer edges.

"When it was molten it pulled that way and then it hardened."

Harold replied:

"That's very interesting Ms. Yuka, very interesting."

He began to picture a planet that was all hostesses. He thought he could be the head of the hostess union on this planet.

The planet would have a trapdoor and the entire inside would be a gigantic wooden room housing thousands and thousands of hostesses waiting to be sent to restaurants on the earth.

All of them young and prettier than the other women who worked there and prettier than 97% of the customers. Apparently there was some unwritten rule about this.

Harold tried to stay in the present in the classroom, he focused hard but the dream on the moon was drawing him back even though it wasn't doing anything. But he fought it.

He looked ahead at Elizabeth's plastic barrette and he knew that it was made from oil.

Maybe the oil from the eyelash of a brontosaurus. No— that could probably make 100,000 of them.

Little did Elizabeth know that perhaps there was part of a dinosaur on her head.

Maybe he should raise his hand.

"Yes Harold?"

"I don't mean to alarm you but I think there's a good chance there's a very small amount of a dinosaur on Elizabeth's head.

"Although I do think it looks very becoming. And it doesn't seem to be causing a problem."

But he didn't.

He smiled thinking the world was such a fascinating interesting place and all he or anyone had to do to enjoy it was to be awake.

Chapter 15

Now he was back to the moon dream.

He noticed something moving off to the right in the distance. It appeared to be a little person walking down the hill toward the water.

The hill looked like a dune on Cape Cod except it was grey and it was on the moon.

The person stopped and seemed to put some things down onto the beach. They were about 100 yards away.

Harold wished that he had his grandfather's telescope. Or Warren's.

A rare HaKii Notris bird which is half Japanese and half Chinese flew majestically through the rectangle. This was an extremely unusual bird in the sense that not only was it two species combined, one of the species had gone extinct.

The dark green and black feathers had a metallic shine to them, like a repainted Camaro from the late '60s.

This bird caused Harold to think about a girl in his class named Christie who would raise her hand and ask to go to the bathroom even though she didn't really need to go.

Then when she got in there she would go into one of the stalls, sit down and start crying.

Ms. Yuka eventually figured out what was happening. It

turned out she was doing this because she realized someday her dog would be dead and it made her very sad.

Quietly he sat in the Adirondack chair made of sand on the peaceful moon. Relaxed as if he were taking a bath. A couple of thoughts came across his mind with no birds involved.

They were images that he wanted to remember to paint when he was back in Ms. Yuka's class.

The first one was of 3 horses standing beside each other just looking at a merry-go-round about 30' away. It was all in a big field of green grass out in nature with no sign of civilization around.

The second thought was a painting of a pool of blood with a diving board.

The person off to the right now seemed to sit down on the beach. It appeared to be maybe a blonde haired girl.

Elizabeth perhaps?

He felt two different things about it. Part of him wanted it to be her but another part of him wanted it to be another girl.

"It's always fun to be around a different girl."

His grandfather told him while in bed delirious from a fever.

Harold was standing beside the bed.

His grandfather was moving his hands quickly as if he were knitting very fast.

"You'll look so good in a turtleneck Harold, really so good. By the way in case you're wondering I do not have malaria."

Blankly the boy looked at the old man whom he loved very much.

At the time Harold did not know what he was talking about but a few months later after learning the meaning of the word he would name the neighbors' dog Malaria.

The neighbors didn't know that. He would only call the dog by that name when he saw him and he and the dog were alone. The dog's real name was Tiffany.

Harold figured that the dog spent more time alone than he did. The big difference being going to school.

Although Harold thought this could be argued because he felt like he was alone even sitting with the 30 other kids and Ms. Yuka.

The person was too far away to know for sure but seemed like a girl sitting with her knees pulled up toward her with her arms crossed resting on them.

If Harold was on the witness stand in a trial and being questioned about whether the person in the distance was a boy or a girl he knew the lawyer would whittle down his conclusion to the person "just seemed" like a girl.

Harold saw lawyers as fact whittlers. Different lawyers would whittle the facts into different little wooden sculptures of some kind of meaning depending on what suited them best.

The concept of a lawyer defending a murderer and getting him off even though he knew the person had committed the crime fascinated, horrified and infuriated Harold.

When thinking of whether or not there was a God this was definitely in the column of no God.

However, he thought, maybe if there was a God, he's thinking a couple of steps ahead of him.

He smiled to himself about the idea of "maybe God is thinking a couple of steps ahead of him," if there was a God.

Perhaps God was waiting for the lawyer to die and then be right in front of him, standing sheepishly in his presence.

God would then say to the lawyer: "I'm going to ask you a question and I would like you to give me a yes or no answer.

"Did you or did you not while you were alive make a lot of money getting people off who you knew had committed murder?"

The lawyer's little lawyer mind would be racing knowing that God already knew the answer. Just like he learned in scum law school to never ask a question that you don't already know the answer to.

But this was that concept times infinity, times the expansion of the universe, times the speed of light and the concept of light and everything else that ever existed and would ever exist. If there was a God.

But in this situation there is a God. A God sitting right there talking to him.

After his thoughts circled around and around and around, like cesspool water going down a drain, he would conclude that he should just say yes and hope for mercy.

The lawyer looked up at God who was now eating a Granny Smith apple and said:

"Yes."

Taking another noisy bite of the apple Harold imagined that God would make a small motion with his hand—like a king in the movies sitting on a throne.

Then a couple of men would come in and take the lawyer to a big stone room that had a very large slicer like in a deli except the round blade would be about 8' in diameter.

They would then insert the live lawyer into the stainless steel movable shelf, just like the ones in the deli.

The two men would happily slice the screaming lawyer into very very thin slices like 90 year old Mrs. Emmet Thomas of Vermont likes her baloney.

Then they would open the door in the floor and with a whisk broom sweep his thin remains through the hole and they would fall back to the earth in dirty alleys where the rats would refuse to eat him because of their higher sense of humanity and he would just rot away.

This same scenario would happen to Johnnie Cochran, Alan Dershowitz, F. Lee Bailey, Robert Shapiro, Barry Scheck, Carl Douglas, Jose Baez and thousands of other pieces of shit that someone gave names to when they were babies.

Harold wondered if the person in the distance had brought a book to read at the beach.

He remembered that his grandfather told him that he once went to the beach and forgot to bring a book so he wrote one.

It was about a city that accidentally hires a roller coaster company instead of a subway company.

It's all underground and at each station it's flat and looks just like a regular subway. Then when the people get on and the train leaves the station it's a whole other story.

Harold looked back at the beautiful, beautiful earth and then over to the probably girl sitting in the distance.

Since he could barely see her he decided to take advantage of this and fill in the details however he wanted.

Which was also how he figured the Bible was written.

He decided she would be wearing a dark straw hat with her sandy blonde shoulder length hair hanging down. And a red one-piece bathing suit with white shorts on.

The grey moon dune she was sitting on had some of that tall green grass like in Wellfleet, Massachusetts.

Because Harold had no coffee to drink he didn't have enough enthusiasm to make the girl be someone else and decided she would just have to be Elizabeth.

But he did have an intergalactic crush on her.

He thought maybe that's why some people just settle on marrying someone, because there was no more coffee around.

Suddenly something way off in the sky caught his attention— moving quickly coming from the opposite direction of the ocean.

A saucer shaped spaceship.

Seemingly choosing a location, hovering a thousand feet in the air above where the girl was sitting.

He judged it was about 100' in diameter and 35' from the top to the bottom. Just like in the 1950s movies.

No sound was coming from it or if there was he couldn't hear it.

Slowly this surreal-looking machine descended straight down stopping about 80' above the surface of the moon.

Twenty years later when Harold was in Amsterdam he would remember this exact moment of the dream while eating a piece of chocolate cake loaded with hash.

The thought would be brought to him by a rare Iguana Blue Bird drifting through the rectangle whistling the Louis Armstrong song:

"What a Wonderful World."

Nothing happened for 30 seconds. Then a black square under the spaceship opened and silently unfolding all the way down to the surface of the moon was a wicker staircase that stopped about 15' behind the girl.

Apparently when touching the surface it made a small noise because she turned around.

She stood up and her little girl earth brain processed what she was seeing.

The sound of waves and seagulls and a buoy could be heard even though there were no seagulls or buoys.

Chapter 16

To her the staircase looked like the skeleton of an escalator.

She seemed like she was deciding whether to go up or not.

Then to Harold's artificial astonishment the girl turned and looked right at him. They stared at each other for about 10 seconds.

She walked back to where she was before and sat down.

The long wicker staircase retracted back up into the spaceship like the tentacle of an octopus and then came right back down as if it was just stretching.

Harold got up out of his Adirondack chair made of sand and started walking toward the girl and the spaceship 100 yards away.

It was a peaceful walk, quiet, no temperature, the beautiful blue marble 238,900 miles in the distance.

He had many thoughts along the way one of which was brought by the following bird:

An all white Leopard Whale bird that only existed in Sweden for 35 years starting in the early 1400s and reminded Harold of something he read in Dr. Christmas's waiting room.

It was a story about a scientist named H. Tracy Hall who invented synthetic diamonds.

He used a powerful hydraulic press on carbon and then heated it to 5,000 degrees Fahrenheit to mimic what the earth would do naturally.

The article said they became extremely useful in the aerospace and stone-quarrying industries and they continue to use them today in making drill bits, grinding machines and saw blades.

At the time H. Tracy Hall worked for General Electric and the company made a huge amount of money from his discovery. They gave him a $10 savings bond.

As Harold continued walking he thought of asking Elizabeth to marry him and then if she said yes giving her a synthetic diamond engagement ring.

Even at 7 years old he realized the layers of psychological meaning this would have.

Somehow he thought it would be like someone buying a ticket for the *Titanic* and then ending up on the *Carpathia* which was the ship that came many hours later to pick up the *Titanic* survivors. Or the opposite of that.

Another thought was birdless. He imagined a little recently adopted orphan boy in Tibet who could hear colors.

He might say:

"Mama, listen to how blue the sky is today! Listen to those big white clouds! One of them sounds like the shape of a dog! Do you think so too!?" The boy could also see fine.

Halfway to Elizabeth and the spaceship there was a small wooden table. Harold saw it in what was the distance at the time.

On the table was a little bit larger than normal white ceramic coffee cup full of black coffee that looked hot.

Harold was so happy and excited and suspicious.

He decided to drink it—who would poison him in his own dream anyway?

He sipped it because it was hot, his hand on his hip, stood there and looked around.

"This is great," he thought. "What are the chances of a hot cup of coffee on the moon?"

As he looked to the earth the coffee entered his system. He wondered how many priests were down there. He thought of the little white square on the priest collar.

The coffee was picking up speed now like the horses rounding the first turn in the Preakness, the one Secretariat was in.

He thought the white square looked like a little movie screen and wouldn't it be great to project a movie right on there.

On every one of them at once. All of a sudden shots of helicopters in the sky are playing on all the priest collars in the world.

Someone would be in the confessional and then from behind the screen where the priest is, slowly getting louder and louder comes that very distinct sound of US helicopters in Vietnam.

"Bless me Father for you have sinned."

Sipping more coffee Harold continued walking.

A bird flew through the rectangle so quickly it cannot be described.

It went too fast to really know what happened. Like everyone's life.

But the thought the bird brought was clear. He wondered if when a person died could that be looked at as they went extinct? That person went extinct. Why not?

As Harold got closer the first thing he noticed was that the spaceship appeared to be made out of plywood. How could that be? Talk about old and new.

This reminded him of a painting he wanted to do which was of a Horse-Drawn 747.

Yes it was plywood painted white. If he didn't know it was true he wouldn't have believed it.

The girl he thought was Elizabeth turned her head toward him. It did seem to be her but something was different.

Maybe it was her but a year older than she really was.

Which reminded him of his idea about a guy who invents a special pair of glasses that can see three minutes into the future. In case he wanted to change his mind about something.

The Coffee the Coffee the Coffee running through his brain.

Blasted on caffeine a hummingbird whips through the rectangle causing Harold to wonder when they stopped putting "The End" on movies and why?

Could it be that the people who made movies realized that the people who were watching the movies would know when it was over? Could that be?

He got to where the girl was and stopped. She was sitting on her towel with her dark colored straw hat on and she looked up at him.

"Hello Elizabeth—you are Elizabeth right?"

"Probably Harold, do you want it to be me?"

"Um, well, I'm not really sure. My grandfather once said—oh never mind."

"Is that the grandfather that you talk about in class sometimes? He lives in Maine on a lake?"

"Yes. How do you like being on the moon?"

"It's nice."

"That's it?"

"Well I didn't know there would be an ocean and a lighthouse or a spaceship. Actually the spaceship is the least weirdest thing here."

He looked up the wicker staircase and saw that it went into darkness.

"You know part of me thinks that you being in my dream is kind of pushy."

She stared at him with her girl eyes. He took another hit, I mean sip, of coffee.

Then he said, "Not really. Do you want to go up these wicker stairs into the white plywood spaceship on the moon?"

"Yes I would like to."

There was no sound coming from the spaceship but it was different than just quiet. It was almost like it was pumping out silence.

Harold thought it was like his idea of a lightbulb that gave off darkness.

This would be good if they were showing a movie in the class and no matter what they did, still some light came in through the blinds.

"Well I think we should just to see. It can't be dangerous because this isn't really happening, so the worst that could happen would be synthetic danger."

She smiled and he noticed the little dimples that weren't there before as she said:

"Ok, let's try it."

Elizabeth stood up and Harold with his hand motioned up the staircase and said:

"Girls first in case there's danger. I'm just kidding."

"Well even if you think you're just kidding the fact just under the surface of a comment like that is the real truth."

Harold knew she was right and decided not to bring up his connection between women going first and the canaries in the mine shafts.

As they went up the wicker staircase it made that distinct sound that wicker chairs make when you sit in them but even more. The staircase had some give to it like a rope footbridge.

The two of them stopped about halfway up to take in the view. Harold didn't see Anthony but he knew he was in the vicinity.

When they looked back up they saw a man standing at the top in the entrance to the spaceship looking down at them. Harold recognized him immediately.

It was Carl Sagan. He absolutely knew it was him.

"Harold, there's a man up there."

"I know."

"Maybe we shouldn't go."

Now Carl Sagan was motioning for them to come up. The world-renowned astronomer from Cornell University was dressed like Harold thought he would be dressed.

Dark brown tweed jacket, white button-down shirt, black pants.

And on his feet, ballet slippers. Maybe.

"Harold, I think that's Carl Sagan. For a minute I thought he was wearing ballet slippers. He wants us to go up, what do you think?"

"I guess so."

Before Harold moved he looked around to take another look at the view.

The beautiful ocean on the moon that looked yellow for some reason.

It might have been the way the light from the sun was being bent from the gravity of the moon. Or it could be just because it was in his dream.

The earth way in the distance. He turned around the other way to the huge cliff with the beautiful old lighthouse/church at the top.

He then realized that having a memory of a dream was a double piece of information about something that never happened.

He felt the mind was amazing.

He also wasn't sure what were the flaws and what weren't. He was in 3rd grade.

They continued to the top.

"Hello there, little earth children on the moon."

He said this with a big smile while reaching his hand out to greet them and help them into the spaceship.

"Hello I'm Harold."

"Hi my name is Elizabeth."

"You're Carl Sagan right?"

"Yes I am Carl Sagan, very nice to meet you. Come on in."

They walked into a gigantically large circular room with a dark wood floor. A mixture of light and dark color knots in them.

Like a farmhouse would have.

Directly across the room was a huge stone fireplace that appeared to go up into the ceiling.

The opening was 5' wide and arched 6' tall. Like in a ski lodge.

A good medium size casual fire was going. There were several candles around and what appeared to be kerosene lamps attached to the walls about eye level.

All this gave the inside of the spaceship an orange hue look to it. Not like the spaceships in the movies.

In this giant room there were only a few pieces of furniture.

Two Adirondack chairs facing the fireplace. Randomly placed a couple of straight back chairs that looked like they were rocking chairs but they weren't.

There was also a rectangular table made of a light colored wood with one chair at the end. The matching chair was in the middle of the room with a guitar on a stand next to it.

The table had a few books on it and some notebooks.

The place had that fire burning smell that reminded Harold of his grandfather and the house at Moosehead Lake. And Tinga.

They all walked into the room. It was quiet, extra quiet, synthetic silence.

Harold was looking all around, he noticed about 10 paintings on the walls spread all the way around.

Inside Harold was overwhelmed by the situation but tried to be as casual as he could be.

Carl walked them toward the fireplace.

There the three of them stood. Their inner instinct machines feeling out the situation.

Both Harold and Elizabeth felt like they possibly liked Carl.

Carl also felt like he liked these two children.

The boy had no idea what to say but was rescued at the last second by a dark blue Trident Chickadee whipping through the rectangle.

As far as Harold was concerned the nuclear Trident submarine would be named after this bird. For what reason he did not know. The bird brought Harold the following questions.

"Mr. Sagan, how fast can this spaceship go?"

"It can go 1 second slower than the speed of light which is . . ."

"Yes, 186,000 miles a second. I know that nothing can go faster than that."

"Well we could actually go faster but we don't often do it for a couple of reasons.

"One is we don't want to make the speed of light jealous.

"The other reason is that if we went that fast and some scientists on the earth happened to notice then almost every calculation in the history of the world would be thrown off and it would just be so very stressful to all of humanity.

"So we only gun this thing when we're so far away that it can't be detected from the earth."

Harold looked away from Carl to the fire, delaying the two questions already manufactured in his head like a Ford assembly line that had been retooled to make sentences instead of cars.

"A couple of things—when you say 'we' could go faster does that mean there's other people on this spaceship besides you?

"And I didn't know that something like the speed of light—a nonliving thing—could get jealous? Unless you're just joking."

Before Carl could answer Harold noticed on the right side of the mantel a small circular birdcage about 8" tall and 4" in diameter. The bird in it looked like a sparrow but it was all yellow.

It winked at Harold but Harold did not wink back, there was something he didn't like about the bird. He thought when Carl Sagan wasn't looking he would give the bird the finger.

He also noticed what appeared to be a little tiny doorbell to the left of the door to the cage.

In the background of all this mixed into the silence perfectly and gently was the beautiful sound of the ocean—just going and going and going like a liquid heart that never stopped.

Harold prayed that this dream would just keep going like the ocean.

"Well Hank.

"It's Harold."

"Oh yes sorry. Well Harold, I always say 'we' because it makes me feel less lonely. No there is nobody else here.

"And yes the speed of light does have feelings. Not all non-living things do but light does. I think that's why it goes so fast—it doesn't want to get involved."

Harold looked over at Elizabeth who was now sitting in one of the Adirondack chairs looking at the fire. Her blonde hair had an orange glow to it because of the jealous light from the fire.

Harold was puzzled and needed to sit down.

"Mr. Sagan, do you mind if I sit down?"

"No not at all. And please call me Carl. Would you two like some water?"

They both responded, "Yes please."

"It's good it's $H_{16}O$."

The yellow bird now appeared to be smiling. Not at anybody just like he was thinking about something.

Harold was having a chain reaction of thoughts crashing into each other like a 20 car pileup.

He thought that maybe Carl Sagan was insane but he always loved him and never felt he was insane, which meant it was he himself who was making a crazy version of him because it was his own dream.

Harold couldn't believe he was meeting Carl Sagan even if it was when he was sleeping.

He remembered something his grandfather told him about the Lakota and dreams.

The Lakota Legend says that the good dreams go through the center hole to the sleeping person and that bad dreams get caught in a web then perish in the dawn's light.

Harold felt that this was definitely a good dream. He also thought that maybe this dream seemed so long because it was approaching the speed of light.

As Harold sat down he remembered what he read on the wall of a bathroom at a Texaco station in Greenville, Maine. It said: *The closer something gets to the speed of light, the slower time goes. It* was signed *Al.*

So in temporary conclusion Harold figured because of what the Lakota said and what Einstein said he was having a very good and very long dream.

Harold thought of a classmate in school named Tim and how he used to say to him, "The only difference between you and time is the letter *e.*"

Carl came back with two glasses of water and handed one to Harold and one to Elizabeth.

She said, "Thank you. Mr. Sagan, let me ask you something— why is this spaceship made of wood?" She was 7.

"Because wood is extremely durable, more than people

think. A lot of planes in WWII were made of wood. And the boats that landed at Normandy.

"And Howard Hughes's plane the *Spruce Goose*, which is still the biggest aircraft ever built, was made mainly of birch wood and some spruce. It flew once during a test for one mile."

Harold had another idea for a painting which was an aerial view of the birch trees near Moosehead Lake with the shape of the *Spruce Goose* made in missing trees. Like a cartoon silhouette.

Harold still called them cartoons refusing to use the word *animation* because he thought it was pretentious.

"We used birch trees cut down near a lake in Maine."

Another painting of an aerial view of a forest near Moosehead Lake in Maine with a 100' diameter circle of missing trees. Like in a cartoon.

Elizabeth looked at Carl Sagan and said:

"If the fire is constantly moving how does it affect the light being thrown from it?"

"It doesn't, the light is going so fast it has no effect."

Then Carl took out of his pocket and unfolded a small papier-mâché accordion and threw it in the fire. It immediately burst into flames.

"You see the light from the burning accordion it's all going the same speed. A match, a flashlight, the sun."

Harold looked at Carl and said:

"I've seen *The Pale Blue Dot* picture. That's such a great idea you had of turning the camera around on the *Voyager* to take a photo of the earth."

He learned of this while reading a *Reader's Digest* in the waiting room of Dr. Christmas's office, of course.

"Thank you, Harold. And what do you think of when you see it?"

Carl Sagan was now eating out of a bag of Lay's potato chips.

"A few things. First of all it makes me nervous. Because it seems like the earth and everyone on it is floating in the middle of nowhere. It's like 3½ billion people are stuck on an elevator that can never be fixed."

"Interesting," said Carl as he offered the chips to Harold and Elizabeth.

"It also causes me not to be able to keep things in perspective."

"I see what you mean, Harold. That's why I said I use the word 'we' before because ever since that picture was taken I feel alone.

"Not lonely, but definitely alone. It also makes me laugh when I hear people say they need some 'alone time.'"

Harold was smiling at Carl and said:

"Yes I guess that picture makes that hilarious."

"That's correct, Harold."

Then out of his pocket Carl Sagan took out a small wallet size laminated picture of *The Pale Blue Dot*, the earth surrounded by universe, and handed it to the boy. "I want you to have this, Harold."

Then he took out another one and gave it to Elizabeth. "And you too, Elizabeth."

They both thanked him very much.

Harold thought to himself he will always remember this moment even though it wasn't really happening.

He also thought that if anyone ever asked him if he had a picture of his home he could just show them that.

Carl bent down and put another log on the fire.

Harold gave the finger to the bird.

The beautiful sound of the ocean continued outside.

Chapter 17

He was looking at the wallet size picture of *The Pale Blue Dot*, the little tiny tiny earth a half of a pixel and the overall flukiness of life even starting on the earth and then him even existing and it caused a giant amount of emotion in the boy.

Suddenly Harold got tears in his eyes because he was overwhelmed with how happy he was to be alive.

The bird also had tears in his eyes because Harold had just given him the finger. He was a sissy bird.

Carl walked over and sat at the chair with the guitar. He picked it up and he was fiddling with it.

Harold and Elizabeth stayed where they were in front of the fire but they turned their heads toward him.

Because the giant round room had wooden floors and high curved ceilings and was almost completely empty it would give a reverb to the sound of the guitar if Carl played a song, which he did.

"In the old days before complicated high-tech recording studios they might have a musician sit in an empty stairwell and run a microphone out there to record him because the sound bounces around nicely.

"That's what this room is like except it's in a wooden spaceship on the moon."

Then he laughed loudly and madly for 5 seconds like a guy in an insane asylum in a '50s movie.

Harold and Elizabeth were looking at him with small smiles. Fascinated and maybe a little bit frightened.

"I would like to play you a song about all of life and the ending of life. It's called 'Everybody's Going.'"

Carl Sagan began playing a slow three chord song with a delicate beautiful melody.

These are the lyrics he sang—

it's almost over now and
time to go
everybody's leaving fast
and slow
doesn't matter what you
do or what you know
there's darkness in the
light that's in the sky
there's darkness in the
light that's in your eyes
why don't you turn around and
wave goodbye
wave goodbye
wave goodbye
you can't believe you
were a baby how can that
be?

everything has changed
everything you see
if that is true then anything
can happen
and it does
and it will
and it shall
nothing's still
why don't you turn around and
wave goodbye
wave goodbye
wave goodbye

During this Harold thought he saw Ms. Yuka standing in the doorway playing the violin beautifully along to the song but he wasn't sure.

Anthony was standing on the floor beside her wearing a tuxedo with tails. He was looking up at her and watching.

Carl put the guitar back in the stand, came over and put another piece of wood on the fire.

Elizabeth looked very relaxed sitting in the Adirondack chair.

"Mr. Sagan, did you write that song? It's very nice even though it's serious and sad."

"Like my first wife. Kidding, yes I did write it so I guess that means that Harold wrote it. And Elizabeth, please call me Carl."

She smiled.

"Yes I wrote it on the piano but I don't play the piano so I always play it on the guitar."

"Harold, I didn't know you played the guitar—you never mentioned it in class. What made you write that song?"

He thought this but didn't say it:

"Elizabeth, if you knew everything about me you'd shit all over yourself."

But he said:

"Nothing. I was thinking about how short life is and then I drank some coffee."

Carl Sagan joyfully stood there in front of the stone fireplace smelling that very distinct fire burning smell looking at his two elementary school guests in his wooden spaceship.

The sound of the ocean in the background. He was thinking what a nice moment this is. He was thinking—"Thank you Harold, thank you."

Harold was now looking up at the yellow bird in the cage on the mantel but he wasn't really focused on it.

Carl said:

"Harold, what are you thinking about?"

"I'm wondering if somehow the speed of light has an effect on how fast a broken heart mends."

Elizabeth looked at Harold when he said this but Harold kept looking at the bird.

Carl watched them and wondered if they liked each other in that special way that most often ends up like being in a plane crash.

"Yes go on Harold."

He said it like a professor would say it to a student encouraging him to make his point.

Like in one of those wooden type theater lecture rooms in England or Austria in the early 1900s.

Harold could feel Elizabeth looking at him.

He continued—

"Well if everything in the universe is made up of the same small list of elements then there must be light in the makeup of the human body too.

"So I'm wondering if that can have an effect on the quickness of the healing of a broken heart."

"Hmmm. I'm not sure. I'm thinking maybe it could. You know what?

"It has to have an effect it must. It's so obvious."

He said this as he offered more potato chips to Harold and Elizabeth.

They both took some and said thank you.

"Harold, let me ask you this, and I think I know the answer, have you ever had a broken heart?"

"No but I know it's coming. Like rain, it's always going to rain sometime."

Harold looked back at the bird on the mantel, then he imagined the all white eagle that just flew through the rectangle in his head breaking into the cage and ripping him to shreds.

Carl continued:

"Come over here I want to show you something."

They got up and walked with him across the very large oval shaped synthetically quiet room to two French doors.

The great wood burning smell was very comforting to Harold.

It made him feel at home even though he was on the moon.

He needed coffee desperately.

Carl opened the two French doors which went out to a large wooden deck.

The three of them walked out. The view was amazing off the spaceship silently hovering 100' up.

Very clearly the earth could be seen way in the distance. In this distance.

There were no railings. About 5 birds flew by casually.

Elizabeth stood staring and then said to Carl Sagan—

"Is this the biggest spaceship in the world?"

"Well not in the world because we're not in the world. You know what I mean."

"Yes I know what you mean and the answer is no. There are some that are 3 times the size of this one."

"Really? Have they ever flown over the earth? I mean has anybody ever seen them?"

"People think they've seen them but they never have. They've seen the results of them flying over but they don't connect it to the spaceships."

"Really like what?" said the little pretty blonde haired girl in her red one-piece bathing suit and white shorts and extra white teeth with waves crashing and the cliffs and the light-house/church in the distance.

"Well one thing they started doing several years ago was these giant spaceships traveling across the universe when passing by will just take a very extremely large shit onto the earth without even slowing down. We know them as malls."

With her sparkly blue eyes the 7 year old said:

"Really that's what malls are?"

Before Carl could answer Harold asked:

"Do they shit anything else onto the earth?"

"Yes, many many years ago a huge spaceship took one of the biggest shits they've ever taken onto the earth, it's the city of Los Angeles."

Chapter 18

Ms. Yuka: "Does anyone know what astronomy is?"

Little Brenda's brain tells her she knows and to raise her hand.

"Yes Brenda?"

"Something to do with the stars?"

"Yes it's the study of the stars and the universe. The universe is the endless world of space and stars. Does anyone know who Carl Sagan is?"

Harold random thought:

A mother who tells her kids if they are ever injured they should bleed internally so they don't mess up the place.

Harold imagined himself raising his hand and saying—

"Yes I know Carl Sagan, I spent time with him on the moon. He's a very nice person. A tall man. Very tall.

"He gave Elizabeth and I a small laminated wallet version of his famous picture *The Pale Blue Dot*.

"We spoke of how the speed of light can affect the mending of a broken heart. He played Elizabeth and I a song on the guitar called 'Everybody's Going.'

"We were just standing on the deck when I stopped thinking about the dream and now I'm here again. Even though I only went away in my mind."

Harold thought that would be a good name for a song—
"I Only Went Away in My Mind."

But he didn't say anything. Nobody said anything.

Ms. Yuka continued:

"He's a famous astronomer who writes books about the universe that regular people like us can understand."

Harold was looking past Ms. Yuka to the poster on the wall behind her that had pyramids and one of those giant Egyptian heads on the sand.

He remembered seeing a show on TV of anthropologists opening tombs in Egypt and how the bones of a body were all twisted with rags wrapped around them.

And the rags were probably nice clothes when the person was buried and how since the person died thousands of years ago somehow people think they're not as important or they don't matter as much as people who are alive now.

It was clear to Harold that he and everyone he knew were someday going to be like that.

This doesn't just happen to other people. There are no other people. We are the other people.

He imagined being at the beach seeing a single engine plane pulling a sign—

THERE ARE NO OTHER PEOPLE, WE ARE THE OTHER PEOPLE

A plane that flew all over the world endlessly.

Powered from the energy of people wondering if there was perpetual motion.

For a second Harold imagined Carl Sagan making out with Ms. Yuka and her saying:

"Oh Carl baby Carl baby."

He was amused and thankful that the human mind did so much on its own.

Harold thought that maybe he should make a list of all the things he never imagined before. He made a note of that in one of his notebooks.

He decided to leave the classroom and go back to remembering his dream. Very quietly under his breath he said:

"Bye-bye."

Carl said to Harold and Elizabeth:

"Come here and walk to the edge of the deck even though it has no railing."

He walked over and sat down at the edge but neither Elizabeth or Harold moved.

In two seconds Harold had the following thoughts without trying to have them—

Running and pushing Carl Sagan off the deck. Running and pushing Carl Sagan off the edge while holding Elizabeth's hand and flinging her off at the same time.

Or not pushing Carl Sagan off but grabbing Elizabeth's hand stepping quickly to the edge and flinging her off just to see his reaction.

Harold thought that some people probably lived their whole lives just for other people's reaction.

Like everybody who's ever been in show business.

Then Elizabeth and Harold joined Carl. They all sat there with their feet dangling over like three Huckleberry Finns except many many differences. Many many.

Harold wondered if there was a huge abandoned factory in Carl Sagan's head. 50 times bigger than the one in his own head.

With millions of genius birds flying all over the place.

The little girl said:

"Mr. Sagan, I mean Carl, could I ask you some questions?"

"Yes of course."

"If the days on the earth are measured by the time it takes to spin toward the sun and a year is measured by going around the sun how would time be measured if you were far away in space and not near the sun?

"And wouldn't it be great if the earth didn't just stay in this area going around and around and instead traveled on and on throughout the galaxy? Think of how different that would be? Talk about traveling.

"I mean right now it's like the earth is just going around at the end of a cul-de-sac.

"Like a toy train on a track. Imagine what it would be like if the earth could go straight out there?"

She pointed out to the universe with her outstretched blonde arm and her blonde finger.

Because when Harold's sister was learning how to ride a bike without training wheels she fell off and chipped her tooth Harold knew the answer to the time question and it had to do with the vibrations of crystals.

By the way, Mary Lu was the name of Harold's sister.

A bright red cardinal that was wearing a tiny St. Louis Cardinals baseball hat, just to be sarcastic, glided through the rectangle, smelling of whiskey, whistling the song "Mr. Bojangles."

The version done by the great musician David Bromberg.

This bird brought to Harold the thought of not saying he knew the answer.

Carl looked down at the little girl sitting next to him.

"Well Elizabeth, one way to measure time without the sun would be with the vibrations of crystals.

"And yes if the earth traveled through space that would be quite extraordinary. That's an idea I've never heard of before. Quite fascinating."

Instead Harold thought of telling him about a painting he once did of a boy holding the end of a rope that looped up into the air and a little girl standing under it about to jump up when it came back down.

The little girl had black braids and was wearing a faded red summer dress and white ankle socks and green shoes.

The shoes were the kind that had a strap that went over the top of her foot. She was happy and smiling and you could see that it was summertime.

The disturbing thing about the painting was that the other end of the rope went up and over a branch of a tree and there was a man hanging there dead.

She had her back to the tree and the dead man. It was a big beautiful maple tree like one that would be in Concord, Mass., the town that Walden Pond is in.

The title of the painting was

The Happy Little Girl.

It was very very colorful. Harold had done it in saltwater colors.

As far as life he always thought that the colors alone were worth being alive for.

But Harold didn't tell Carl Sagan about the painting and didn't ask him if there was an abandoned factory full of birds in his head.

Instead the three of them sat on the deck listening to the waves of the ocean and looking up at all the stars.

Not all the stars, the stars that they could see.

It occurred to Harold that never again after elementary school would he sit in a room full of children watching someone talk for 6 hours a day and have no rights and no say.

A complete legal dictatorship in a country founded upon and based upon not having a dictatorship.

He would never be in this situation again unless he was in prison or he continued going to school.

The little boy didn't know what would happen in his life but I did.

By the way Harold's first words were: "Your witness."

His parents didn't know where he would have learned these words but they didn't think much about it.

The ocean on the moon continued with its trademark sound as they sat silently other than the circus inside each of their heads.

Harold curiously said, "Carl is this spaceship transporting anything?"

"Well, funny you should ask, Harold, yes it is. In the lower level there are a number of merry-go-round horses, about 500 of them. They're very very beautiful."

Elizabeth looked up at Mr. Sagan and asked:

"What's the difference between a carousel and a merry-go-round?"

Harold knew the answer because of a routine six-month teeth cleaning.

"Well Elizabeth the difference is the direction that they turn. In the United States the merry-go-rounds turn counter-clockwise and in Europe the carousels, as they're called, go clockwise."

"Why is that?"

Said the pretty very very smart blonde girl who years later would send several men to their emotional deaths.

"I don't know," said the world-renowned astronomer.

"But there must be a reason I would imagine."

The birds in the abandoned factory in the boy's head were getting all excited, flying in and out and all around, moving quickly like when they fire that gun off at the end of a runway at an airport so the birds don't get sucked into the engine and cause a disaster.

Several birds went through the rectangle one right after another, I don't have time to describe them.

One went through the rectangle causing Harold to remember something he learned at the planetarium field trip which was that the northern hemisphere of the earth also turns counterclockwise.

Naturally he then imagined millions and millions of merry-go-round horses going around the earth that is spinning 1000 miles an hour.

Going around right at the equator. He figured they would be at an altitude of 80,000', which is where outer space starts.

Well where it starts in reference if you were standing on the earth.

Nobody knows where outer space starts except for God— if there is a God.

The horses would all be beautifully painted with their heads turning left and right flying like wingless Pegasuses.

Chapter 19

Harold thought this would be a good painting and wondered if there should be kids on the horses.

Carl Sagan then offered some coffee to Harold and Elizabeth but she didn't want any so he gave her some $H_{16}O$.

Harold drank his and her coffee which caused the following ideas and mood.

He thought instead there should be no kids on them because he didn't feel like spending the rest of his childhood painting children on wooden horses that are almost in outer space.

And furthermore he'll call them carousel horses if he feels like it and doesn't give a shit which way Carl Sagan says they're going—Fuck him and clockwise and fucking counter-clockwise.

He was sick of Carl Sagan's shit. Harold was experiencing a caffeine induced rage.

Maybe because the coffee was made with $H_{16}O$. Maybe not.

Harold remembered the story his grandfather told him about when he was doing the survey in South Dakota. He and three of his Lakota friends were out in the middle of a field looking at an abandoned merry-go-round.

The Lakota were on horseback and had recently eaten some peyote. They were looking at the merry-go-round and laughing so hard they almost pissed themselves and fell off their horses.

The three of them were yelling at each other in Lakota while they were screaming laughing.

His grandfather could only remember one thing they were saying which was: "No Wakan Tanka, No Wakan Tanka," meaning "Godless, Godless."

"Carl where are you bringing the horses?" said the small girl.

"I'm bringing them to God."

"Oh wow really? Why?"

"Well Elizabeth because when God was a little boy he didn't have many toys and he didn't play many games, so it just seems like the right thing to do.

"And although he didn't ask me directly, I've never talked to God and would never go around saying I did, but I feel it, I just feel that God would want to see some beautiful merry-go-round horses.

"To see something that wasn't there in his childhood.

"I just think that having someone bring them right to him would make him feel good.

"Because I don't think he has a lot of things done for him. And I think that God might even be a little bit lonely.

"Elizabeth imagine how stressful it would be if a lot of people were constantly wondering if you existed or not?

"And were questioning your behavior?"

Harold thought he heard Ms. Yuka telling Brian Owens that he could not go to the bathroom but he wasn't sure.

He did think he had one thing in common with the idea of questioning the existence of God, he questioned his own existence.

Right now he wasn't sure about anything. He had to take a deep breath, shut his eyes and think about things for a second.

He was exhausted and had to get his bearings.

Then he remembered a thought he had recently which was that a painting of a real horse and a painting of a merry-go-round horse were both fake versions of horses even though they were based on two entirely different realities.

Which made Harold wonder if that was the same as believing whether there was a God or not.

Elizabeth smiled at Carl Sagan and said:

"I think that is so nice of you. And you want to know something? I know there is a God because my mother told me there is."

Right then Harold heard Ms. Yuka yelling:

"Brian stop that and go to the bathroom right now!"

Brian was standing at the side of the class where the windows were, pissing into an aquarium that had a snapping turtle in it.

The turtle's name was Clicky Harrelson. His first name was

because he always made a clicking sound with his mouth. His last name was because that was his last name.

Carl smiled at her as if she was showing him a rare penny where Lincoln is facing forward.

Harold thought that Carl Sagan should be on the penny.

When Harold heard Elizabeth say why she knew there was a God he thought of the huge amount of information told to children by their mothers.

Part of him thought they should all go to prison. Not that some of the information wasn't valid.

Harold simply thought the power a mother had over a child was so exponential and unreal and that it should be illegal.

He would grow up to question all authority and had already started.

I don't know if you noticed or not but in this story he hardly mentions his own mother.

That in itself is a reverse announcement.

He looked down at the beach from the deck of the spaceship.

The beautiful ocean that continued all the way to the moon's horizon.

Past the horizon was the black velvet darkness where sitting, floating was the blue and white earth which from that distance was about the size of a marble.

Beyond the earth were thousands and thousands and thousands of tiny stars.

Harold knew his brain was way out of its league in regards to the universe.

The traveling starlight was just one of the many concepts in life he had to block out because it was just too hard to understand. It confused everything.

He looked to his right. Carl and Elizabeth were sitting there with their feet over the edge of the deck.

They were now playing two concertinas, little accordions like from the time of the Civil War.

What were they playing?

The hit song "Spanish Eyes" by Al Martino.

Harold noticed Anthony standing at the far end of the deck quietly singing along. He was wearing a Merle Haggard T-shirt.

The bird cast a small shadow of himself onto the wooden deck.

Harold wondered if something could cast a shadow of something other than itself.

Chapter 20

Of course the amount Harold didn't know was way more than the amount he would ever know. That's why he was happy most of the time.

The boy on the moon was then startled by a noise.

It was like a spinning noise that was getting faster and faster then leveled off.

Somehow it sounded like a powerful breeze in the distance but it was coming from in the ship, from underneath.

"Was that the engine starting up?" asked Elizabeth.

Carl looked at her as he ate some more potato chips.

"Yes Elizabeth it is."

"Are you going somewhere now?"

"Yes, in a short time I have to continue on further into the Milky Way."

Too bad Elizabeth was not having this dream instead of being in it because I'm sure she would have liked to experience when she asked:

"Is that where God is, is God in the Milky Way?"

"No he's not there but he has an office there."

"You would think it was an abstract office, very strange and surreal, but it isn't it's just a regular office."

Her eyes sparkled like two empty Rolling Rock bottles if they were blue instead of green.

"Well, it must be a pretty big office if you're going to put 500 merry-go-round horses in there."

"Yes it's a huge office with no furniture and just a phone on the floor near one of the walls. It's the size of an airplane hangar."

Harold was listening and watching Carl and Elizabeth.

He was wondering if people have a feeling when they're in somebody else's dream even if they're never told about it.

"I'm leaving them there and he can come and get them whenever he wants."

"Carl let me ask you something?"

"Yes Harold."

He wanted to ask him if he was insane taking 500 merry-go-round horses to God and leaving them inside his office in the Milky Way—but he couldn't do it.

He didn't want to make him feel bad. Also he really knew it was himself anyway but he pushed that aside and because of how fast the mind worked he thought of two other questions to ask instead.

The first was did he think rocking horses were baby merry-go-round horses? He ruled that out because of how ridiculous it was. So he asked him the second one.

"Carl before you go do have any advice to give me and Elizabeth since we're so young and little?"

Elizabeth smiled at Harold but he didn't see her because he was looking at Carl.

Which was good because then he didn't have to spend time and energy wondering what that smile meant.

"Yes my advice to you is to take risks in your life—that's the best thing I can tell you. And I don't mean something like walking across a highway blindfolded.

"When I was in junior high I had a part-time summer job at the Walter Mackenzie Planetarium in Nova Scotia.

"I would change the lightbulbs that were the stars. That's how I first got interested in astronomy.

"I worked my way up to that job and first had to change the bulbs in the lobby.

"In fact now whenever I'm in a lobby and look up at the lights in the ceiling I can make out a simple solar system.

"My father wanted me to be an electrician but from working at the planetarium I got it in my head that I would love to be an astronomer even though I thought it would never really happen.

"Like a kid wanting be a baseball player or an astronaut. Although I couldn't really want to be an astronaut because when I was a kid there were no astronauts.

"But at least I wanted to try. Because I thought what if I end up being 50 years old selling insurance in Wyoming and always wondering what would have happened if I had tried it.

"Not that there's anything wrong with selling insurance in Wyoming.

"So I took the risk to pursue being an astronomer and I've had this whole life and career because of it.

"That little tiny fork in the road changed everything."

The two children listened intently then Harold said:

"Did your father want you to be an electrician because he was one?"

"No he wasn't one, just kidding—yes he was. In fact he's the one who did the wiring in the planetarium I worked at that's how I got the job."

"Why didn't he want you to be an astronomer?"

Said the wingless little blonde girl that God made in a billionth of a second in his spare time. If there was a God.

"He thought it was an unrealistic situation and didn't understand how you could get paid from thinking about things that were so far away."

Ms. Yuka was now standing at the blackboard in front of a large screen she had pulled down that had pictures of dinosaurs all over it.

She was saying that the brontosaurus was the biggest animal to walk the earth.

Harold knew that whales were the biggest animals ever, which fascinated him and he wasn't sure why. It had something to do with that they lived in the ocean.

And he liked that not only were they the biggest they were still here.

As he looked at the pictures he focused on the Tyrannosaurus rex and how short his arms were.

He thought it would be impossible for that animal to masturbate.

Maybe that's why he looked so furious. Harold thought

that God must have done that on purpose as a joke, just to amuse himself.

"Before I get going come with me."

He motioned for them to follow him with the same finger he would use to dial the phone to call NASA to suggest that they turn the *Voyager 1* spacecraft around and take a picture of the earth before it was too far away.

The pale blue dot.

They followed the tall genius inside to an elevator and took it down 3 floors below to where the giant warehouse was.

When the doors opened they saw what appeared to be a stationary herd of very colorful wooden horses with 6' silver poles going right through them at the base of the neck and coming out between the front legs.

If you didn't know what they were for it looked like a huge tray of horse hors d'oeuvres.

The colors were very bright and shiny and the eyes so real it seemed like they might blink.

"I like the red ones the best," said Elizabeth as she stood in the warehouse of a spaceship on the moon.

"Yes the red ones are very beautiful I agree. They all are. I really like the black ones and the green ones," said Mr. Sagan.

"What do you think caused you to have the feeling to bring these to God?" said the boy.

"Well Harold, I was looking at a postcard of the painting *The Last Supper* and in front of Matthew there is a chalice and I thought I noticed in the reflection a dog lying on the floor in front of the table but I couldn't really be sure but something else I did notice and was sure of was that out the window behind Jesus and the apostles were two horses standing in a field.

"This small fact stuck in my head for years and years and years. So a very long time later when I was going around in my spaceship to here and there I came upon these merry-go-round horses and I thought to myself, 'Yes, I must bring these to God.'

"Are you wondering where I found them?"

As he held out an open bag of potato chips.

"Yes."

"I can't remember where I got them, I've just been to so many places."

"I love that painting and I've looked at it many many times."

"I figured you liked it, Harold."

Harold knew the painting well and was sure there were no horses seen out a window behind Jesus.

He kept this to himself because he felt that Carl Sagan might be so out of his mind that he could be dangerous.

"Was the person who sent the postcard traveling in Italy?" said the little girl.

"No she was in a bookstore in Hartford, Connecticut."

"Carl, think of this. Can you hear me?"

"Yes Harold."

"Imagine if there is a God and he believes there are people but he's never seen them and he isn't really sure and he just had to be faithful that there is. Imagine that."

"Yes very interesting Harold. But God would know there were people because God knows everything."

"That's your opinion," he mumbled on purpose.

"What?"

"Nothing."

"Harold you kill me."

"I'm serious."

"I know you are, but it's still hilarious."

After admiring the 500 merry-go-round horses Carl walked the children to the wicker staircase down to the surface of the moon.

They stood there awkwardly. They liked each other. They were sad to say goodbye.

The dream ending reminded Harold of the sadness of when the summer ends.

For Harold or any boy or girl the summer seemed close to a year long.

Harold now saw that Red Cloud, the great leader of the Sioux Nation, was standing off to the side and a few steps behind Carl Sagan.

He tilted his head back to look up at the stars and take it all in.

When the boy looked back he thought he saw Red Cloud and Charles Bukowski tickling each other and giggling.

His first thought was he hoped his room in the insane asylum would have a window.

"Well kids I really liked meeting you and enjoyed our conversation but it's time for me to hit the road. I have to travel 20 million light-years by Friday.

"Harold I guess I'll be seeing you again if this becomes a reoccurring dream. And you too Elizabeth."

"That would be great," said Harold.

"I hope so very much," said the girl with an IQ of 256.

Carl handed Harold and Elizabeth each a bag of potato chips.

He then walked up to the top of the staircase turned around in the doorway and yelled down, "Remember, take risks!"

For the rest of his life whenever Harold ate potato chips he would think of Carl Sagan on the moon.

Pleasantly on this sunny day Ms. Yuka asked the class:

"Does anyone have an unusual dream that they would like to share with the class?"

No one raised their hand. Then Brenda O'Hearne did.

"I had a dream it was a very hot summer day and my dog was made of wax and we had to keep him from going outside otherwise he would melt."

"Very interesting Brenda, thank you for sharing that. Anyone else?"

A bird that looked like Al Jolson if Al Jolson looked like Mariel Hemingway drifted through the rectangle with a sneaky look on his face which caused Harold to raise his hand.

"Yes, Harold."

"I had a dream I was on the moon with Carl Sagan."

"Ok what happened?"

"Many things, we talked about merry-go-round horses and the painting *The Last Supper*. There was also a waitress named Tinga working on the moon."

She had no reaction and moved on.

Chapter 21

Ms. Yuka was now pointing at the green blackboard with a wooden pointer that had a black rubber tip.

She was pointing at the word *premises* and Harold didn't know why because he wasn't paying attention.

He focused on the wood of the wooden pointer which caused him to think of two things.

One was a drawing he once saw in a book of Michelangelo painting the Sistine Chapel.

Harold was very taken by the huge wooden staging that was built in order for the genius man to be 68' up to do his work.

The other thought was wouldn't it be great if when he was finished someone took the large amount of staging and built a small house out of it?

Harold thought he would love to live in that house. How magical that would be?

He was imagining being in the house lying in his little bed in his little bedroom and looking up at the ceiling.

He imagined doing a painting of the basement on the ceiling.

He was in a deep trance when all of a sudden Ms. Yuka said:

"Harold could you please put the word *premises* in a sentence."

His immediate response in his head was, "Rather than in a sentence I'd like to put it in your ass."

But he really said:

"While Michelangelo painted the Sistine Chapel he didn't want anyone else on the premises."

"That's very good Harold."

He pictured her at night tied up and strapped to the mast of a burning pirate ship.

A full moon. Calm seas.

Stunningly beautiful quiet long shot, all darkness other than the moon, the flames and the screams.

The screaming from that distance sounded like a cat on its honeymoon.

Ms. Yuka was now mentioning that everyone had to write a one page paper about the stars.

Anything they wanted to write about them.

"You have 3 days to write it. Are there any questions? Yes Harold?"

"Does God have a last name?"

Before she could answer he continued:

"Or maybe God is his last name so I wonder what his first name is?"

She smiled at him with her black eyes then ignored him.

She wished she had vertical pupils like the devil or a goat.

She was so sick of his shit and wished that when the weather got warmer he would just evaporate or melt like Brenda's dog.

Harold was very interested and almost obsessed with the universe. As are lots of children his age.

Then in time this interest usually wears off for most people.

But it wouldn't for Harold. Or Carl Sagan or Neil deGrasse Tyson or Bugs Bunny.

As far as he was concerned, the problem with understanding the universe was the evolution level that the human mind happened to be in at this time in history.

And not only the mind also the sensory mechanics that were available to human beings.

The mechanics that brought the information into the mind. The eyes, ears, sense of smell, sense of touch. And the operation of the brain.

Completely accidental that we are alive when the brain functions like this.

The boy felt that these factors hugely influenced all knowledge of the universe before anything was even looked at.

Moving across Ms. Yuka was a burst of light because a gap opened up in the clouds affecting the sunlight in the classroom.

To see this Harold was using his human boy eyes whose construction and development was given to him by an infinite amount of flukes.

A bird, perhaps the bird known as an Epiphany Eagle, related to the American Eagle, but not through blood but by adoption, glided through the rectangle.

Bringing the thought that since everything keeps changing maybe God himself is actually in a stage of development, like evolution and everything else.

And that fact alone would and will affect everything that has ever existed. If there is a God.

Harold took out one of his favorite pens and a small drawing notebook.

He wrote:

To Ms. Yuka or whom it may concern:

I love to look up and see the beautiful mysterious stars in the night sky.

Like a friendly dog the sun is my favorite star. Probably because it's the closest.

However I must move on.

My God! Maybe God himself is in a constant state of change, and always has been.

An endless state of development and evolution.

And as far as the origin of the universe in regards to religion and science I also believe that God created the Big Bang in order to confuse people and for his own amusement.

He sits there eating Raisinets watching the humans squirm with anxiousness and worry trying to understand it all.

I also feel that God is selfish, if there is a God, and that Mother Nature is a slut. But I do like the stars he made.

The End.

Dec 3, 1965

By Harold

The slut part was just for his amusement.

Chapter 22

When Harold was 37 his grandmother passed away. His mother's mother.

That time Harold walked into the house and she was in the living room straightening pillows.

But it was just to be doing something.

She turned around briefly and said something meaningless and small just to say something but the look on her face said everything that could ever be said.

That moment would be burned into Harold's head for the rest of his life.

Certain quick moments with a huge impact. Internally documented forever in the head museum.

But that would be many years from now.

Harold looked around the room at all his classmates sitting at their desks and all the maps and all the pictures on the walls and all the drawings they did with their signed names thumbtacked on the bulletin board and the big green blackboard in the front of the room with things written on it in white chalk by Ms. Yuka standing there facing them saying many many

many things to help them survive the unrequested journey that they and she herself were all on.

Then after 13.8 billion years and the 3:00 bell the school day ended, Harold got on the bus to go home.

He always sat in the same seat about ¾ back, row 11 on the right.

Both to and from school he sat there, which enabled him to see both views that the fluke festival had provided.

On the ride home sometimes he would play a little game in his mind wondering where his mother would be when he walked in.

Lots of times she would be in the kitchen.

At his stop he got off then walked across the street to cut through the neighbor's backyard, which was on an incline, until he came to the bottom of his driveway.

Once again using the geometry of the situation to go the most direct route.

He walked up the 3 steps to the back door went into the house took a quick right and was now in the kitchen.

His mother was at the sink, a dish towel over her right shoulder with her back to him.

Without turning around she said, "Hi Harold."

He was standing there looking at her and said, "Hi."

Then she said, "How was school?"

And he said, "Good."

Acknowledgments

A special thank you and appreciation to John Ten Eyck, Tim Sarkes, Sean Manning for the tremendous unwavering support and focus, Jonathan Karp, Paul D'Oliveira, Dean Parisot, Bob Lazarus, Mike Goldsmith and coffee.